CaTastrophicAlly CoNsequenTial

STEPHEN C. BIRD

DEDICATION

This book is dedicated to The God of my Understanding, the Intergalactic Force, the Cosmic Creator, the Cosmos, the Great Spirit, the Universe, the Hawk-Headed Goddess, Maya Hiyuh Powuh, Lord Szczmawg, Gütrüne Neuschwanstein, Gunther Glückwünsch, and the Anonymous Dominant Self-Doubting Voice.

ACKNOWLEDGMENTS

All of You are my Yin Yang, my Chiaro-Scuro, my White Clown-Augusto, my Heaven / Hell, my Limbo / Purgatory, my Wood Between the Worlds, my Lantern Waste, my Narnia, my Mordor, my Black and White-Faced Captain Kirk. All of my Childhood Heroes, both those who will remain forever in my Subconscious, as well as those that have become Irrelevant, retain equal validity within the Great Chain of Being.

TABLE OF CONTENTS

HOME SWEET HOME
SILENCE GOLDEN

PART I

An aggressive twelve-year-old Blonde Boy stands outside the front ground level living room window on the north facing side of the suburban, two story split level 1960 Colonial. Then suddenly he is inside the living room. A Brunette Boy, whose friends at school jokingly refer to him as Karole Brunette approaches the Blonde. The two of them are standing at the bottom of the stairway to the second floor; the stairway lies directly behind the front door to the house. Then the Blonde and the Brunette are going up the stairs; the Brunette is holding on tightly to the Blonde. The Brunette Boy knows that if he releases the Blonde

Boy from his grasp, the Blonde Boy will fight him to the death. The Blonde threatens the Brunette with a knife; the Brunette wishes he were stronger than the Blonde. The Brunette Boy looks back down towards the foot of the stairs and sees another boy—the Other Boy. The Other is holding the Brunette's father hostage. Then the Other Boy is leading the Brunette Boy's father away from the bedroom at the north end of the hallway on the second floor. The Other has a gun to the Brunette's father's head. The Brunette Boy is trying to wrap something around the Blonde Boy's head; the Brunette is in a panic. Because to take his hands off the Blonde is to risk certain death. Then the Brunette Boy wakes up, as the Silver Brunette Man, and is banging his head against the bedroom wall of his New York City apartment.

PART II

The Brunette Boy is sleeping on the couch in the living room of the same two story split level Colonial already described. He is thirteen years old. The couch is a dark bronze mustard color, densely woven and irritating to the skin. The living room is full of earth colors, of the kind that were typical of suburban interiors in the 1970's. Besides dark bronze mustard, there is beige, tan, brick red, brown, and an armchair--upholstered in bright orange and yellow hues--that sticks out like a sore thumb. It is dark in the living room; it is night. The Brunette wakes up to see a cylinder of light about six feet in diameter coming up from the living room floor. When the Brunette looks beyond the area of this glow, he sees a being that resembles the god Mercury. This Mercury has silvery pewter graphite colored skin; his face is masculine and sinister. The Mercury unfolds his arms, moves towards the Brunette Boy and scares the hell out of him. The Brunette shuts his eyes in fear, and once he finally works up the nerve to open them up, the Brunette Boy, who is now the Silver Brunette Man, is awake.

LORD SZCZMAWG

And so Lord Szczmawg, Abstractly Patriarchal and Possibly Feminist Ruler of Sky and Earth, bent over, placed his head between his legs to survey the inhabitants of the Blue Green Planet with benevolent compassion, and farted tremendously onto the Gulf of Mecks-Sicko. After doing so, he made the following thunderous pronouncement: *Let there be one million times the amount of methane, one million times above the acceptable level of safety for humans, in these waters. And let this methane proliferate and kill off all the sea creatures of this area. And thus a dead zone will be created, a black hole in the sea, into which all light and life will disappear, to be trapped forever. Asphalt from continuous oil spills will settle on the sea floor, adding yet another poisonous element to the creation of the dead zone. Toxic compounds will evaporate into the air, compounding the pollution already created by fluorocarbons …..*

After the methane-filled oceans of the Blue Green Planet had burned away in a series of fiery explosions, Gothra Schvulkopf walked along the bottom of a canyon, on what once had been the floor of the sea. Due to her skills as a billionairesse entrepreneur, she had managed to gain access to all of the Blue Green Planet's water supply, over which she had complete control. *The Buck Stops Here!* she shouted gleefully, her voice echoing in the empty canyon. *Whoever fucks with me, goes thirsty …..*

Oh look! It's the corpse of Ray-Kill Wraith. Like most humans, she didn't survive the Great Ocean Boil-Off of 2014 (as was predicted by Maya Hiyuh Powuh). I think she was the last of those cooking-show bitches that tried to outdo me. Oh my God! I mean, oh my Great Spirit! What a laugh! Her product line was SO not diversified. How deplorable that she chose to give in to her animal nature! She was Shiva the Erotick, whereas I am Shiva the Ascetick. Sexual suppression will always help one to sharpen one's focus, especially in the Used-to-Be Puritanickal Waning Protestant Work Ethick Post-WASP Upper Echelons of Korporate Olympia. Where are all those people? Did they die in the Dead Zone? Did they finally get what they deserved? After all, I am like Athena who sprung fully formed from the head of Zeus. Yes, it was indeed an Immackulate Konception, and therefore I suffer from no baggage of Original Sin. And so there is no need for me to feel any guilt about any of those jealous competitive wannabe cooking show dominatrices of the Universe, who died dehydrated and gasping for breath just yards away from my Poe-Land Bling-Bling warehouse. It is a testament to their tenacity and perseverance that they almost made it. Yet like Tantalus, ultimately they passed on unsatisfied. It's funny to me, thinking of them being so close to that water; it was just out of reach, at arm's length. ALAS! I WON'T GO THERE! NO TIME FOR COMPASSION! FORGET IT! I GAVE UP THAT EMOTION LONG AGO. Hopefully the respective reincarnations of those pseudo-cooking show bitches will bring them fulfillment. Tough luck girls! Winner takes all! That's Das Kapital-izm! Even though I was raised Katholick, I blocked out its messages, just as I refused to listen to my father barking orders over the intercom he had installed in my teenage bedroom. As a young undergraduate at Barnyard College, I yearned above all to gain access to the floor plan of the Vatican Bank, which finally occurred a decade later after my relentless study of the film "Mysshun Imposs-Sybil VII". All the riches that I absconded supported the creation of my vast array of consumer-friendly products. The story of my big break--of how I attained the Gaymart contract--was a myth created by my Baab-Makkie-Uh-Vellyan public relations staff. Doors started to open for me once I moved my headquarters to Hellystone Park, Amurycka Profunda. Under the auspices of two internationally renowned financial titans, Pluto von Polyphemus and Poseidon Advensher fer sher, I shot to the top of the charts in the Cooking with The Stars world of Sometime Slutty Homo Ekonomicks Dominatrices. Years ago I looked into my crystal ball and saw the protesters at Fuck-You-Pie Downfall Street. Upon seeing them, I said to myself: the members of this movement, and of all similar and simultaneously occurring movements, will be my next demographick. Here on the bedrock of the former Atlantys, I will build new products from scratch, turn the remaining population of the Blue Green Planet into consumers, and civilization will flourish once again. I may be evil, but I have always had the interests of humankind in my cross hairs. I will now descend into the deep meandering aqua rabbit hole of a high contrast landscape dominated by ultra-white birches, to meet the Zalphagamorian, a bronze-colored creature with scaly marbleized hide; and Zauberfeuer, a hedonist resembling the Ghost of Christmas Present. They will escort me to K-Hole Slut Rehab, a nightclub owned by Fräulein Baikalskaya. There I will undergo my orientation that will prepare me for my meeting with Pluto von Polyphemus and Poseidon Advensher fer sher, as negotiating with these two monumental movers and shakers is always demanding and stressful. Preparation is key! At the end of our business, as a reward, my Pumpkin Trolls will stuff my bare ass into a chilled pot of gold at the end of a black and white rainbow. And now ….. down the deep, meandering aqua rabbit hole I GOOOOOOOOOOO !!!! …..

In the meantime, Pluto von Polyphemus, the Opposite Entity from Lord Szczmawg, belches out thick gray black smoke from a volcano twenty-two thousand feet under the sea. This is his warning from Die Unterwelt. The Entity Opposing Lord Szczmawg, Poseidon Advenszczur fer sher, shall have a Blonde Boy by his side, a Cumbrian slave known as Garic from the time of the human Jah-Hee-Zeus. Said Garic shall be constantly castigated for any expression of happiness that enlightens his visage. And Poseidon Advenszczur fer sher shall give Garic a smack on his melancholy mug for each *regard de coquette*, and these words shall Garic hear from Poseidon Advenszczur fer sher:

"NICE GOOD BOY NEVER MAD! NICE GOOD BOY KEEP DEAD PAN FACE FOR DEAD ZONE DEAD SEA SPACE, WHERE ALL CORAL IS DESTROYED BY BUBBLES OF CARBON DIOXIDE! NICE GOOD BOY KEY WEST ICE QUEEN! NICE GOOD BOY NEVER PRECOCIOUS! NICE GOOD BOY ONLY HAS PHANTASM IN TEENAGE MIASMA! NICE GOOD BOY STAY IN PHANTASM, BECAUSE PHANTASM BETTER THAN REALITY! NICE GOOD BOY SUFFER! OTHERS LAUGH AT NICE GOOD BOY'S SUFFERING! ALL EROTIC ATTRACTIONS AND TRANSACTIONS FOR NICE GOOD BOY GOING FORWARD WILL BE COMPLICATED WITH MISUNDERSTANDING, MIS-

COMMUNICATION, HUMILIATION AND ABUSE! POST-SCRIPT: MAYBE NICE GOOD BOY NOT SO NICE, AND HE BRINGS MISFORTUNE UPON HIMSELF!"

Poseidon Advenszcur fer sher lives with Garic in Jean Cocteau's *Orphic Underworld*. They are the new hot couple in the neighborhood, and they enjoy lounging around in beatnik cafes, putting on artistic airs, and sipping extremely dry red wines, recommended by the sommelier who always hides in the bathroom when fights break out between rival gangs of badass bikers. Pluto von Polyphemus steals Garic from Poseidon Advenszczur fer sher, and Garic is taken to the subterranean region below Ye Olde Unfaithful, Gateway to the *Orphic Underworld*, in Hellystone Park, Amurycka Profunda. Believe it or not, this situation has its advantages. In the *Orphic Underworld* beneath Hellystone Park, Garic is surrounded by a harem of He-Queens of a Certain Age who worship him from afar while he looks upon them with unfeigned indifference. Pluto von Polyphemus is constructing a supercollider beneath Hellystone Park. Hopefully, the magma beneath Hellystone will interact with the anti-matter created by the supercollider, to destroy the Blue Green

Planet. This dream of Pluto von Polyphemus suits Garic well, as Garic is Anti-Love and lives only for Pure Sensation. Garic lives for today, never thinking of tomorrow, ignoring the beauty of all sunsets.

During cataclysmic events yet to come, Garic will observe people self-immolating and spontaneously combusting, houses exploding, factories becoming fuel for a chain reaction of massive fires, and he will feel nothing. Garic dreams only of destruction; he never speaks, he always looks straight ahead and he is never any fun at parties. No therapist will ever cure him; the only solution would be the removal of his reptile brain. When Garic laughs, the sound is harsh; it makes one jump. He has a cold look in his eyes, and meets any and all gazes of consternation with a special joy, that only one who cares for no human can feel.

DÜMMERSPRACHE
DÜMMERF@KKER

Usns been speakin duh Dumbspeak uh reel long time now, evuh since dey wuz Gooderz an Badderz. Jes so youse know, deah two kinds uh Dumbspeak. Deah dat dats duh Gooderz speak, an deah dat dats duh Badderz speak. Duh Badderz speak uh version datz all murkie twistie kreepie; Badderz speak dey Dumbspeak so konfusin tuh each udder, dat sometimes evun dey dunt know what dey sayin tuh each udder! But Badcerz speak uh Dumbspeak so mean, nasty, cruel an violent dat dey meanin, even if Gooderz dunt like it, are alwayzies clear on uh way down low primitive level at least. An heah what Gooderz say bout duh Badderz: *Keep yuh friendsiez close--Keep yuh enemeesiez closer!* Badderz think

15

dat dey ain't gots tuh be responsibibble for nuttin dat dey says! Badderz thinks dat dey alwaysiez right bout evurthin! Badderz say dat Gooderz speak duh Dümmersprache, an dat Gooderz be Dümmerf@kkerz! An Gooderz dey say duh same thing bout duh Badderz! But worse den bot sides am dem Evilangelists, uh pipple datz alwaysiez mad cuz dey alwaysiez gots tuh be worshippin dey Jah-Hee-Zeus; themmerz can't have no funsiez cuz dey alwaysiez think duh Jah-Hee-Zeus watchin themmerz! Themmerz alwaysiez parrynoid! An Evilangelists be strange cuz dey watch so much pornographick DVDsiez dat dey can't likewise have no reel sex no mo!

Gooderz an Badderz believes dat dey has duh right tuh die howevuh dey wants; wit Diabeeterz, Pneumeunyeur, AIDSiez; even wit uh gun tuh dey heads! Bot Gooderz an Badderz dunt like no Libbeyral, cuz dem Libbeyralz worship duh Hawk Headed-Goddess, Maya Hiyuh Powuh, Lord Szczmawg an udder Druidyck-Wyckan-Pagan mythologistickal gods. Dem Evilangelists am uh pipple more religiougistickal den bot Gooderz or Badderz. Gooderz an Badderz still like dey Jah-Hee-Zeus principibples, but not in such an alwayzies churchified way, takin duh Holie Ghostie wit em twenty-four seven. In terms of unifickaytion an gettin pipplez together, heah gozie: Gooderz, Badderz an Evilangelists alike has made it dey goal tuh keep all dem Ayrabyckal nations on duh map uh duh Blue Green Planet unduh surveillance. Don't get me wrong; themmerz sher likes dey one hundred percent Ayrabyckal coffee! Dem Brownerz sher am good at makin dat! As long as themmerz leaves all duh brown in duh coffee wheah it should be, an not ovuh heah in Amurycka Profunda! I say brownsiez good in poo poo, dirt, coffee an chocolate, but not on pipplez! Gooderz, Badderz an Evilangelists all wunts tuh know duh wheahabouts uh all dem Brownerz datz facin Murka five times uh dayzie; facin uh slightly more stranger Abrahamystyckal God, dat jes dunt seem quite sensibibble tuh pipplez of Northerner Europapean an Amurycka Profundan origin. Thermmerz dunt like no spirits dat come from blayzin desertie places, or from hot djzhunglie places; only Brownerz worship themmerz.

Gooderz an Badderz worships Swyng Out Sinister Klaas, uh white Doucheyfied Kryss Kryngle cuz hims all jolly rolly poly an ain't no Dizzynyssyan Disckord Kreatin Monster uh Chaos. Evilangelists hates duh Shiva Kreator Destroyer; on second thought, thermmerz likes duh ascetick side uh Shiva, but not duh erotick side, cuz dat dunt have nuthin tuh do wit no Watchtower Paradise Afterlife, wheah pipplez dat believes in Family Values stroll hand in hand, but not in an affectionate way, nor Jah-Hee-Zeus forbid in an incestuous or homosexual way; dem pipplez jes friendsiez, okay! Themmerz dunt wunt no Libbeyral tellin dem not tuh drink no Hawayyanie Poonchie! Themmerz likes dey Schleetzie beersiez reel good; dey even likes it in dey Wholie Kommunyon Koopzies! Gooderz, Badderz an Evilangelists dunt want no Libbeyral tellin em what dey should eat an drink like sum Nancy Nanny Tranny Granny. Even if dems seven hundert pounds an gots tuh be fork lifted out dey own house, datz dey right. Datz respecabibble. Datz Libeureuhteurian. Jes between you and me: Gooderz, Badderz an Evilangelists am likewise hypocripibibble ..... !

CORE-ANN BURNIN LAIDIE

It all started when usns won duh lotterie up heah in Talullah Hassle. Florider. Usns wons uh bus trip roun Germany (or Doucheyland as themmerz call it ovuh deah) stoppin at uh lottuh beer drinkin parties durin Oktoberfest. And it were also kulchural an high-minded goin tuh cities wheah fancie rich Douchey-lander types live; in Frankenfurter businessmenzies was wearin ties wit faggotty colors. Granted ah pre-fer me country types, ah like duh alpenhornie or led-erfeuerhosen or cowsiez wit bellsiez on. Asides Frank-enfurter, usns stopped in Münszczyn an Doucheldorf too. Hell ah even saw prosties sportin dey wares in nice city streets, ah guessin datz legal deah. Usns didn't go tuh Berlin though, which were alright since ah heard all themmerz am faeries an queersiez, an dey mennerz does strange things wit each udders asses. Hell ah dunt evun use duh word ass, specially not in no Evilangelist potluck churchified supper! Ah think themmerz got entirely too much sex goin on in dem soczsgzialiszt countries! Ah heard all dem faggots got big schwanzies ovuh deah in Doucheyland, so ah guessin dat dey can't control deyselves! Now dat womynz all indiependent now, menzies gots tuh be playin wit each udder. An datz happenin in Amury-cka Profunda too, although Jah-Hee-Zeus forbid not in muh nabberhood! Faggots be called szczwoolzies ovuh deah in Doucheyland; an as far as themmerz is concerndie, I say: hell do what yuh like, ahm uh Libeureuhteurian; jes do yer perversie in sum udder nabberhood!

Deah all types uh Brownerz now in Doucheyland wit dey inszczaalaalaah kulchur, an in Amurycka Pro-funda too. Hopes themmerz dunt go blowdie uppitie roun heah! Guess themmerz gots uh special paradise so themmerz ain't uh skeered tuh die! Dey menzies weah dresses an face Murka when themmerz pray. What the hell's wrong wit Jah-Hee-Zeus, may ah ask? Himmerz too good for themmerz? Jah-Hee-Zeus were reel nice cuz him didn't wunt no laidies; him didn't drink no moonshine; him didn't say no dirtie wordsiez. But dem Brownerz wit dey Core-Ann an dey suicidie bomberz; even dey burkie wearin laidies go blowdie uppitie! Themmerz got dey crazie Alley Babber and dey djzheemeenies 'n magickal lampzies. Datz why ah were so happy tuh hear bout uh Core-Ann Burnin comin up, wheah like-minded pipplez like muhself can have dem uh real good time settin fire tuh sacred Ayrabyckal books!

Ah found me uh half-burndedie Core-Ann in uh rusty trash can near duh abandoned chemickal plant heah in Tallulah Hassle. Me knowed it were uh Core-Ann cuz 't were all goldie on duh outside, an it had funny writin inside. Ah so sorry Turrie Djzhonezies didn't wunt tuh have no Core-Ann Burnin! Datz uh Schäme; ah heard themmerz make uh purtie fyre! Datz okay cuz ah gots me anudder ideer; ah heard it were real nice tuh put uh Core-Ann in duh oven, turn it up tuh four hundred degreesiez, den bake it til it turn all brownzie like uh Browner! When dem edges turn brownzie, jes like uh pie, den it be done!

So since Turrie Djzhonezies didn't wunt tuh have no Core-Ann Burnin, some uh muh churchie-laidie-friendzies an ah decided tuh have one, at duh same time as duh Clauszcz von Barby-Kew ovuh deah at duh Fyremenziez Fieldie. We'll be singin Hellerlooyer an purty Jah-Hee-Zeus hymnzies tuh Himmerz ever-lastin Glörya Höll. So come on down tuh duh Fyremenziez Fieldie for duh Core-Ann Burnin! An put on yer purtie burkie fer sum tanzin! (I were jes bein sarkastyckal deah!) .....

Heahz uh last-minute reminder: we takin our gunsiez case dey any Druidyck-Wyckan-Pagan worshippers down at duh Fyremenziez Fieldie; themmerz duh worst kind uh heatheners. We'll shoot em right deah vigilante-style an it ain't gonna be purtie. Themmerz will get uh bullet right between duh eyesiez. And dem bullets will cook dey brainsiez, which am right appropriate, cuz it's uh cookout after all! Hell, girlie! Jes cuz we worships Jah-Hee-Zeus dunt mean usns alwaysiez gots tuh be all saintlie like Himmerz!

THE ENCHANTED YEARBOOK

Ever since she was five years old, Dar-Not-Lean had been given Unconditional Blundt Cake Love to calm and soothe her, to suppress her tantrums. As a result of this practice, she wanted incrementally larger amounts of Blundt cake, and her parents, Float and Ethereal, were happy to indulge. Float and Ethereal were fashionably trim and fit, and this complemented their swinger lifestyle. They snorted cocaine off black lacquer tables. Dar-Not-Lean's favorite kind of Blundt cake was Bedevilment's Food. As Dar-Not-Lean shoved ever-greater amounts of Blundt cake into her mouth, her parents taunted her until she produced the devastated expression that satisfied their sadistic natures. At that point, they would tease Dar-Not-Lean with even more helpings of Blundt cake:

Dar-Not-Lean would coo and whimper until her parents gave her what she desired. Float and Ethereal could have killed her as a baby, but then they would have missed out on the opportunity to delight in her torture. Besides the fact that they needed something to do during those rocky patches after coming down off the blow. The torture of Dar-Not-Lean filled up a void, especially when the swinger parties didn't live up to their advance billing.

Understandably, Dar-Not-Lean was not happy at Country Crock High School in Aryan Fake, New York, a delightful hamlet full of gingerbread houses that was located halfway between Boresaw and Smellicottville. Her nemesis was Mannequin Streetwalker, a young woman who had achieved sexual maturity ahead of her classmates, and who had made forays into the world of adult sexuality ahead of her peers. Dar-Not-Lean envied what appeared to be Mannequin's exciting, glamourous life as a prostitute / coke whore in local motels. At home sitting on the couch in the wood-paneled basement with the sliding glass door, watching reruns of the original *Star Trek* (1966-1969) Dar-Not-Lean would suck her thumb and rock back and forth, obsessing about her various fears: Mannequin Streetwalker; the crushing pain caused by the constant abuse by her parents; her status as an unpopular student and as an outsider. The over-whelming anxiety caused by this obsession led to depression and a hunger for the comfort of Bedevil-ment's Food Blundt Cake. Dar-Not-Lean would some-times even suck her thumb in homeroom, and when Mannequin spied her doing this, she pulled a battery-operated vibrator out of her purse and began to rub the head of the vibrator into the small of Dar-Not-Lean's back. Dar-Not-Lean was so mortified by this, that she remained speechless and trembling when this happened. Nevertheless, despite her fears, Dar-Not-Lean was an excellent student, the Whoremoa-nia Gangster of her class (Whoremoania Gangster was a character from Che Mary Kay Foul Thyng's *Higher Parterre* series). Whereas Mannequin Stree-walker was failing all of her subjects and would have to later pursue her GED. Mannequin was often high as a kite in homeroom. Dar-Not-Lean, on the other hand, although technically sober and clear-headed, was a crucible of confusion; it would be many years before she realized that she suffered from the effects of bad boundaries. That afternoon, at home on the couch in front of the television, Dar-Not-Lean took a deep breath. Just then, she heard her neighbor, Bobby Chushingura, playing *Alice in Chains'* "Dirt" at ear-splitting volume on his bedroom stereo. And in that moment, Dar-Not-Lean was afraid. Because she didn't even feel safe in her own home.

One afternoon, Ethereal waited in her pine-green 1970 Chevy Nova outside Country Crock High School, to take Dar-Not-Lean to the doctor, who was monitoring Dar-Not-Lean's treatment for diabetes. Ethereal got out of the car to smoke a Newport, when something in the 1966 Pontiac black station wagon hearse parked ahead of her caught her eye. Ethereal, being an experienced voyeur, discreetly peeked into the window of the back seat of the hearse. And who was in there but none other than Mannequin Streetwalker, blowing the captain of the football team. Even though Ethereal was a swinger, she was nonetheless morally and hypocritically repulsed by what she saw. And so Ethereal stuck her head into the open back-seat window and said forcefully, *Stop that right now you sex-worker lookin' high school lady.* Without missing a beat, Mannequin looked up at her and said, *Takes one to know one Djzhaavyeruh Hall-Pass-Banger!* before continuing with the task at hand. Ethereal was stunned; but she had some tricks up her sleeve. She went back to her car to get the blueberry pie she had just bought at Tops supermarket, then returned to the station wagon hearse, looked in the window at Mannequin and said, *Hey.* Mannequin looked up. and Ethereal slammed the blueberry pie into her face. *That'll teach you!* Ethereal exclaimed, before lighting up another Newport and walking back to the Nova. But Mannequin was not about to take any shit. She abandoned fellating the football captain, jumped out of the hearse, and proceeded over to Ethereal, who was smoking behind the steering wheel of the Nova. Mannequin began to pummel Ethereal. However, Ethereal could hold her own well enough, and even if she hadn't been able to, she had another weapon at her disposal. Ethereal reached over to the adjacent seat and picked up a black-indigo-violet yearbook that Dar-Not-Lean had left in the car. Once a year, there was a lottery for one enchanted copy of the year-book. This year, Dar-Not-Lean had been the lucky winner. It was the first time she had ever won any-thing in her life. The tradition of the enchanted year-book had begun in 1930, and had continued down to the present day. Whatever color the yearbook happened to be in a given year, there was always one black-indigo-violet copy, whose powers could be harnessed in an emergency. When used in com-bination with a particular incantation that was writ-ten at the bottom of the back page of the yearbook in small print, the enchanted yearbook became a mortal weapon. The phenomenon of the enchanted yearbook was a highly guarded secret in Aryan Fake; in fact, to speak of it was taboo. Bad things were known to happen to those who chose to discuss it. In addition, the enchanted yearbook acted as if it were possessed of a conscience, in a manner similar to that of the Snorting Koockaigne Hat from Che Mary Kay Foul Thyng's *Higher Parterre* series. It would only destroy those who truly deserved to die, regardless of the intentions of whoever attempted to use it. The enchanted yearbook had a mind of its own. While struggling with Mannequin, Ethereal managed to extract herself from the driver's seat and then to kick Mannequin to the ground, holding the enchanted yearbook in front of her with both arms, and pointing it towards Mannequin. Mannequin grabbed the yearbook and pulled it to her chest. Then Ethereal shouted out the spell: *Hawk-Headed Goddess, Obliteramus!* The yearbook immediately became glowing red hot, searing through Mannequin's blouse, burning through her breasts and then burrowing into her chest. Mannequin was howling; the book could not be removed, as it had become grafted onto her skin and bones. Smoke rose up from the yearbook before it burst into flames, and the fire quickly enveloped and immolated Mannequin as she struggled to stand. She then fell back as she burned white-hot and was quickly reduced to cinders. The process took so little time that the couple of students loitering on the grounds of the school barely heard a yelp. What had once been Mannequin was now a pile of gray-black ashes and a few thin strands of smoke.

Ethereal stared at what remained of Mannequin, relieved. *Well ..... I didn't kill her ..... the book killed her* ..... she said under her breath. Just then Dar-Not-Lean appeared, with a big smile on her face. Perhaps Dar-Not-Lean intuitively knew what had taken place; that her mother, who could be so cruel, had actually destroyed Dar-Not-Lean's nemesis. They both got into the pine green 1970 Chevy Nova without a word. Ethereal put the key into the ignition, started up the car and they drove away.

INCESTUOUS INGRYDD

Across town from Dar-Not-Lean, on Route 77 on the outskirts of Aryan Fake, Incestuous Ingrydd did not think that there was anything wrong with the way things were. She had always been protected from any notion of moral judgment. She had no idea that her life was dysfunctional. She wasn't aware that other lifestyle choices existed. It was the only way she knew. She preferred to stay blindfolded in the dark in the attic room of her family's early 20th century two-story home, with a porch that wrapped around three sides of the house. The house was painted a shade of deep pine green, and was complemented by sea foam green shutters and trim. There was one square window, in the center of the top floor facing the street. In the center of that window, one black indigo violet candle was left constantly burning. Back in the attic, Ingrydd waited patiently, holding her hands in front of herself like paws and panting like a dog. Most of the time she played this role willingly. This was Ingrydd's Blissful Bower, where the eyes of antique dolls seemed to come alive to watch her various encounters as they progressed. She sexually serviced her father, uncles, brothers and cousins. Most of the women in her extended family were frigid, so she became the sexual outlet for the male members of that extended family.

Upon entering her attic abode, either separately or collectively, her suitors would see a shaft of light falling across the *Alice in Chains* poster on the wall in front of them. And this light was always the same. If it wasn't, Ingrydd couldn't perform the necessary services. The men kept her well hydrated so that she was always drooling. The attic was equipped with a full bathroom in which she could shower, douche or give herself an enema, as needed. The men treated her with reverence, like a high priestess of the amourous arts. They never had to be forceful or sadistic. However, this is not to say that Ingrydd always complied. If the men suggested any sexual activity that displeased her, she would take off her blindfold, turn on the overhead light and say ..... *Well, we could do that. But then you would have to die* ..... And with that, she would point to a set of gleaming stainless steel cutlery that rested on the cedar chest beneath the *Alice in Chains* poster.

CODA

Incestuous Ingrydd was the sister of the recently deceased Mannequin Streetwalker. Ingrydd was not the vindictive type, but there was one other sister as well: Hermana Morafin (the three girls were half-sisters with three different fathers). Hermana was the most dangerous and destructive of the three, as well as being a clairvoyant. She had foreseen how Ethereal, mother of Dar-Not-Lean, had destroyed Mannequin Streetwalker (but like Cassandra, Hermana had been unable to prevent the inevitable). And so Hermana Morafin would avenge her dead sister. *Die, Ethereal, Die!!!!* she muttered through gritted teeth nightly, as she lay insomniac on her bed, staring up at the slowly rotating ceiling fan, in a scene resembling one from *Apocalypse Now* that featured Martyn Szczeen.

DJZHEEMI SPARKS
HOMEROOM DAYDREAM

Kate Smith's jolly patriotism struck a chord with the Depression-era residents of Anti-Inter-Continental, Ohio. A town so lily-white that German was considered an ethnicity. Of course this was back in those times when country doctors took chickens for pay. It is hamlets like this one that caused Jack Kerouac to mourn the disappearance of *red brick small towr Amurycka Profunda*. Anti-Inter-Continental, Ohio was the ancestral home of Djzheemi Sparks, a student at West Whoreland High School, West Whoreland, Faerie County, New York. Djzheemi had decided to take volleyball with the girls in Ms. Lossthumous' physical education class that year, because he didn't want to engage in any rough and tumble with the boys. It was 1979, years before the time when men who have sex with men, even the hyper-macho leather types, finally felt comfortable enough to stroll around holding hands in public in cosmopolitan areas. In the words of the immortal Gütrüne Neuschwanstein's poem:

HOMOSEXUAL
MATH
EQUATION

A Queer =
A Faggot =
A Screamer =
And the Sum Total of All Three
= Das Bitch

Gütrüne Neuschwanstein
Sümmer of Lüv, 1967

Djzheemi felt a sadness when he sat in homeroom listening to the gruff, apathetic voice of the principal, Nirvana Dialysis Kiwanis, making announcements about the various sports teams' wins and losses. Hearing those announcements made him want to spike the volleyball that much more ferociously, but only from a passive, kneeling position. Sitting in homeroom, Djzheemi was so anxious about the day; he just wanted to get it over with. *There is absolutely no joy in my life! Where is the joy? Garszcz Damn It!* he intoned. Nirvana Dialysis Kiwanis, droned on. "I am pleased to announce that all participants in the BOCES program (Board of Cooperative Educational Services) have been transferred to a menacing exoplanet whose atmosphere is cooled by means of a jointly created Japanese-German ventilation regulation system." Upon hearing this, Wülfie, the Austrian exchange student, blurted out, *Ja, Japanisch-Deutsch, aber auch Spanisch.* The principal continued. "This year's winner of our Sister County Student Exchange program with Eyjafjallajokull, Iceland is Allison Eckslacks-Wellness. As everyone in West Whoreland knows, the Eckslacks-Wellness family is the wealthiest in our township, and although Allison didn't desire or even deserve this opportunity, due to minimal effort on her part, her father pulled some strings. Her scholastic achievements are mediocre, but she has c well-rounded social life, including fetishistic practices in which one can voyeuristically participate with her. On any given night, she can be found sporting her wares by Pill-Bar, a badass biker dive across from the West Whoreland Tops Supermarket, in outfits inspired by *The Rocky Horror Picture Show*. In these getups, she goes by the vulgar moniker of *Alison "One-L" Shitbox*. To her credit, she is not beyond redemption. She is aggressive and fearless; characteristics well suited to the captain of the field hockey team. That is the role in which she is most at home." The public address system clicked off abruptly, and was followed by a few moments of crackly static; then a Darth Vader-like voice was heard ..... *Last but not least: Iceland--The Dark Horse of the Northern Atlantic; so neglected, underrated, misinterpreted--will finally become a geopolitical force to be reckoned with. When the Apocalypse of Maya Hiyuh Powuh (MAYA = ILLUSION) arrives in 2012, the Survivalists will flock to Iceland, via ethanol-fueled flights on Aeroflot, to engage in Rapa-Nui-style cannibalism, leading to the inevitable auto-annihilation of Iceland's culture and all of its inhabitants .....* The public address system clicked off abruptly once more.

Djzheemi had been working on a poem about his future, of which he was so proud:

THE
MORALLY
SUPERIOR
KOOCKSOOCKER

He wrote a poem on this day

To tell the world that he was gay

He read this poem to some folk

In downtown venue midnight stroke

He read aloud and all was calm

Though later two Jld be dropped a bomb

They stared at him no boo nor hiss

Though neither did they blow a kiss

When he was done he said good night

They rose as if to start a fight

A vicious bitch did then assent

To lecture him; to represent

"We do not like your written work

We think you are a stupid jerk

Go back to your provincial town

Put on your faggot wedding gown

Yes leave New York and don't come back

Accept that you are just a hack"

-- Djzheemi Sparks, 1979

Djzheemi also wrote the following poem that he classified as avant-garde that he was too afraid to read in English Literature class:

ODE TO THE COLOR BROWN

In the Uncensored Beige-Tan-Vomit Universe

Of an X-Rated Willy Wonka

There is a Visual Smorgasbord

Dedicated to the Color Brown

In All of its Wondrous Variations

Of it Little is Spoken

It is in Fact Taboo

It is the Rainbow of Shit

-- Djzheemi Sparks, 1979

Djzheemi was brave enough to read *The Morally Superior Koocksoocker* to his English Literature class. And when he was done, he experienced the Cruel Realism of their Insensitive Laughter. He was so naïve; they ridiculed him for that reason alone. At that moment, Djzheemi decided to change his name to *Puto Das Boot.* As *Puto Das Boot,* he would be loved by all. He became lost in thought as he considered the possibilities ..... *Everything is going to be different once I acquire a wardrobe of rubber fetish gear. No one will even blink an eye in the Future World of Berlin, when two butch guys in vulkanized rubber motorcycle outfits will be able to walk around holding hands. Those badass bikers will be my friends! I'll show these fools of West Whoreland. They're all going to die in this preppy abyss .....*

The Aszczford Livelie Hallow Skulptur Park was the sole repository of culture in the Southern Tier of Faerie County; to Djzheemi, Aszczford Livelie Hallow Skulptur Park was a Druidyck-Wyckan-Pagan shrine. In that regard, Djzheemi reminded himself ..... *And no one can tell me how I define my deity, or what I call him, or how I perform my rites of veneration. If I want to, I can tend my sacred fires in aluminum garbage cans, wear tree branches on my head, worship owls (inspired by Che Mary Kay Foul Thyng's "Higher Parterre" series) or even believe in Eastern godlessness* ..... Djzheemi was enamoured of the Hawk Headed Goddess, whose existence in contemporary life was confirmed to him by her symbolic presence in *Juliet of the Spirits*. In Djzheemi's dream, his friends, who worked at the West Whoreland Tops supermarket, and who spoke with the harsh nasal accent of Western New York, would moon bonfires they had made in Aszczford Livelie Hallow Skulptur Park, releasing their gases into the flames to create a full range of spectral hues! This effect could be heightened by throwing aerosol products--such as *Aqua Net, Sure and Pssssst!*--into the fire as well.

The few friends Djzheemi had at West Whoreland High he referred to as his Sacred yet Bestial Tormentors. They now surrounded him in the smoking lounge, an outside cement-terrace area near the swimming pool, ideal for the likes of Alex and his droogs. On that day, Djzheemi looked wistful, and his Number

One Tormentor, Saydystyck Sayshay, asked him what was wrong. Djzheemi replied, "Sadly, my aunt, the Stalwart yet Effervescent Sofia Niedersachsen of Anti-Inter-Continental, Ohio, has left the Realm of the Living on the Blue Green Planet. I thought I was going to inherit some money from her, and frankly I would have preferred cash. But all she left me was a pair of Ass Pants. "Ass Pants?!?" gasped his Number Two Tormentor, Afraiderycka von Fäg Häg. "Come now my good one; those vestments do sound wondrous strange!" Djzheemi blushed, then dared himself to answer objectively: "Truth be told, they are not actually called Ass Pants; they are referred to in my New York City Future World as *chaps*. They are black leather pants designed to let the bare buttocks show through. I believe that by giving me this gift, my dearly departed aunt, the Stalwart yet Effervescent Sofia, divined the evolution of my interest in fetishistic practices. In faith, I shall never have need of this kind of flambuoyant outerwear. All perversion rises up from deep within, sometimes disguised as sweetness, sometimes as innocence. Fortunately my perversion is metaphysical. I am but a Disinterested Observer. Perhaps I shall sell these chaps on E-Bay in my New York City Future World."

Djzheemi's Number Three Tormentor, Nonny Nameless, piped in. "Forsooth, but I am glad you have no need of these Ass Pants. The children of Amurycka Profunda must be protected from atrocities such as these. I am shocked and amazed by such indecency! Even if it is properly cleaned, it is better for all concerned that the buttocks be covered. I believe that our principal, Nirvana Dialysis Kiwanis, should be made aware of this phenomenon of Ass Pants." Djzheemi piped in. "Oh Nonny, be still with your waxing hysteria. In the Amurycka Profunda Future World, it will only be in the more remote, obscure pockets of the country where such objections will be raised." Nonny spoke again. "What kind of lady was your aunt Sofia to bequeath you these *pantalons abominables*? And is it true that after her one and only husband died, to whom she was married for just one year, she lived as a frustrated closeted lesbian for the remaining forty years of her life? I sincerely hope that thou shalt never sport these Ass Pants, or *chaps,* as you refer to them, in public."

The group split up and proceeded to their respective classes. Djzheemi suddenly realized how furious he was. His Sacred yet Bestial Tormentors would never understand him; all they had to offer was their judgment. They, indeed, are the Morally Superior Koocksoockers! ..... he muttered to himself. Then Djzheemi took a moment to offer a prayer of thanks to Lord Szczmawg. He was grateful that he did not live in a Middle Eastern or North African country with a repressive, reactionary regime where one could be executed if they were found to be in the possession of Ass Pants / *chaps*. Then he hurried off to Ms. Lossthumous' class, and volleyball with the girls.

BOBBY BLUETOOTH

One night at Djzheemi's Comedy Shithole, Gay Ridge, Queers, New York, a woman was heckling Bobby Bluetooth, and it was far from the first time. Boy was he tasteless! And delusional; he fooled himself into thinking that it was just some horny, frustrated broad who was looking for a post-show shag. She was clearly the castrating bitch feminist type that Bobby abhorred. *Are you, or have you ever been, a homosexual, Mr. Bluetooth?* she forcefully enunciated, sounding like an actress playing an attorney on *Law and Order*. She had been listening impatiently to Bobby's series of jokes about two supposedly straight guys who couldn't get laid at their local pickup joint, and ended up going home with each other. The crowd hushed up after the tough bitch's heckle; maybe she was right about Bobby. In that moment, Bobby thought to himself, *Well there was that time with the neighbor boy when I was thirteen.* Then Bobby responded, *Is youse duh Naomi Szczteinham of Gay Ridge, Queers?* Because that was the only name of a prominent feminist that he knew. The crowd didn't know who Naomi Szczteinham was, but they shrieked and applauded like trained seals nonetheless. One woman in the audience asked her husband, *Is Naomi Szczteinham one uh dem hookers dat Szczarlie Szczeen did cocaine wit in uh bathroom szcztall?*

This is how Bobby Bluetooth had been introduced by the emcee fifteen minutes before: "Ladies and germs, our next performer, excuse my f@kkin' elitist liberal French, is such a f@kkin' funny f@kk, I piss my pants every time he opens his mouth; later on they'll be a slide presentation of my wet crotch so youse know I ain't lyin'! Our next funnyman is a favorite at clubs and colleges up and down the Eastern seaboard, although there's a rumour goin' around that he pays for stage time at the Penn Station Dunkin' Donuts, the Starbucks at the corner of 86th Street and 3rd Avenue, and the Port Authority Men's Room! No one can say he isn't dedicated! He works on his craft wherever he can. Like I said, he makes me laugh my f@kkin' ass off. Frankly, if our next performer had a pussy, I'd f@kk him. To put that remark in context, please google *Latent Homosexuality* for the Wikipedia link. And now, without further Mountain Dew, please welcome my very good friend who currently owes me three grand-- Let's have a big hanc for the highly sophisticated, articulate, erudite and refined wit of ..... Bobby Blue-tooth!" (*the crowd goes wild*) .....

Bobby was now standing at the bar at the back of the club, nursing a whisky and soda, happy to have turned around the situation with the brass-balled psycho dyke bitch that had attempted to f@kk with him. The emcee was bringing up the next act: "Our next performer, our next young lady, is a performance artist (*the crowd boos and hisses*). Which means she probably won't be getting any laughs tonight! (*the crowd laughs and cheers*). Now, now; let me finish! Even if I have been disrespectful; do not do as I do, my friends! Yes our next young lesbian can pull things out of her koochie and has even been known to projectile vomit at the end of her set. Just a warning to those of you sitting up front ..... Let's have a nice hand for ..... Szczell Szczocked Szczerry Szczareeya!" (*half-hearted applause from the crowd*) .....

Szczell Szczocked Szczerry Szczareeya approached the mike in a show of false fragility. She was hidden under her black burka and only her hands were visible. She began her act. "Good evening ladies and gentleman. That's right, my name is Szczell Szczocked Szczerry Szczareeya, and here's a multiple-choice question for all of you: I was born into a religion that is neither Christianity, nor Judaism, and yet shares the same concept of Abrahamical monotheism? In other words, if these three religions were the three main branches of a tree, they would share the same Abrahamical trunk? Okay, maybe this isn't a multiple-choice question, but rather a process of deduction? So what religion was I born into? Any wild guesses? What, you think I'm going to stay home all day, hiding in the house, just because I was born into a religion that is neither Christianity nor Judaism, and yet springs from the same root? No f@kkin' way! Is anyone here a Christian? (*no response from the crowd*).

Jah-Hee-Zeus F@kkin' Piss Christ! Now I feel irreverent ….. Here's another multiple-choice question: What happens to a comic when they can no longer mask their impotent rage? Do they punish the audience, even though they know this is not only wrong, but an act of self-sabotage as well ….. *Jah-Hee-Zeus F@kkin' Piss Christ!"* Finally she admitted to herself that she was bombing, but managed to come up with one last zinger: *How about we all get together in the parking lot after the show and burn a rainbow flag? I mean, no matter how much we all hate each other, we all hate faggots even more;* "everyone can agree on that, right?"

Then an outraged woman, who should have been eating oatmeal while waiting for the Last Judgment in Branson, Missouri, stood up and protested: *We don't want yer Browner Ayrabyk P@kki Türki belly-dancin' suicide bomber types heah in our country. Ah fear duh dominoes are uh fallin'! Wish ah had me uh Core-Ann on me right now, so ah could make it go orangie-yellowdie-goldie-burndedie an see duh flames reflected back in dem black eyeballs yer uh hidin' unduh dat black burka! Whatevuh happened tuh all dem purty blue-eyed types heah in Amurycka Profunda?*

But Szczell Szczocked Szczerry Szczareeya cut off the heckler just before she was finished: "You obese diabetic over-medicated ignorant trailer trash couch potato! I stand before you as a professional entertainer in a secular environment. In my country, I was an astrophysicist before the Tallulah-Ban regained their power. What makes you think that you, you irrational mentally challenged Evilangelist, can convince me that the cultivation of the poppy is wrong? My appearance to the contrary, I am fulfilled, and the suffering of the typical 1950's Amurycka Profundan housewife, not counting the occasional breaks provided by Tupperware parties, was nothing compared to yours! I am from a 5,000 year old culture. Whereas all you understand is Pop Tarts and Sara Lee Cheesecake!"

Szczerry started to cry. "I so wanted to share my suicide bomber jokes tonight; I thought they would help to defuse the tension that exists between the West and the Middle East. I wanted to heal our world that now feels the ill effects of our current cultural divide and the geopolitical rift! But instead, what I wish upon all of you now is the combined power of all the curses of Moroccan black magic, the existence of which was confirmed by your Amurycka Profundan expatriate writer, Paul Bowles! *Paul Balls! Get it? He was from Queers! And he was a queer!* What, did that one go over your heads, too? Careful, my friends, you know not with whom you are dealing. I am possessed of the powers of Gillian Bellaver in *The Fury* ....."

At this point, Szczell Szczocked Szczerry Szczareeya was interrupted and dragged from the stage by security. Half of the crowd had departed during her tirade, and the emcee stepped up to engage in damage control, to prevent the rest of the audience from leaving: "Okay everybody, the controversy is over, now we can go back to our lives of noisy desperation, as our very talented radical extremist performance artist from another culture has been handcuffed, sedated and taken to Creedmoor. Okay lazies and gerbils? I think you'll really like our next act. Someone who doesn't want to make waves, someone who just does the good old-fashioned funny. That being said, no one's perfect. Our next performer has been up for thirty-six hours straight playing the slots in Atlantic City. What can I say? He likes to fly by the seat of his pants. He's like the only straight guy in a *Cirque Du Soleil* show. He makes a little extra money on the side servicing *Park Avenue Pearls and Blue Blazer-Type Bitches!* He's also partial to the usage of a special European, Latin American and Japanese toilet called a *bidet!* Lechers and gomorrahs, let's have a nice hand for ..... Tommy Fantasie!" (*the crowd goes wild again*) .....

Tommy Fantasie, a fucked-out, strung-out guy who resembled a combination of Georgie Girl Mikhail and the Four Whores-Men from the *Joisey Shawh* Apockalypse, along with the *joi de vivre* of Bon Temps Jovial, approached the mike with confidence. "Howse youse people doin? Jes so youse know; I go bot ways, I do duh AC / DC. So if youse don't like my jokes, after duh show we can do whatever youse like; sixty-nine, titfuck, up duh ass, double penetration; you pay, I play! No bullshit, I ain't no clock watchin' hustler! I can also getta hold uh my coke-whore, gamblin' partner for uh threesome if desirable. Jes one request, all right? Anal and vaginal douches are mandatory, youse know what I'm sayin'? I keep uh rubber tube in my bathtub in case youse princesses and effeminate passive male freaks need to freshen up. I'm on duh Facebook as Tommy Fantasie; it's duh *Ye Olde Englyshe Leather* spelling! And yes I accept Pay Pal! (*the crowd has been laughing in spite of themselves; there is also talking and murmuring*) ..... Okay jes cuz I ain't no hoity toity sissy bitch dat sticks out his pinky drinkin outta teacup, youse think I gotta dirty mouf? I managed uh crack house! I dropped safes offa roofs in duh Bronx! I beat up faggots wit baseball bats in dark alleys. "And dat was jes foreplay ....."

THE DOWNWARD SPIRAL
OF CINDY CIPRO

It had been yet another day of exhausting ridicule, unwarranted criticism, sharp rebukes, stinging jokes, cruel assessments, unsolicited advice, and mundane conversations. But how could all of that be the fault of Cindy Cipro, who struggled to get up in the morning, just to give the world the finger? Just to say fuck you world? With that kind of attitude, no wonder no one felt any empathy for her. They just felt sorry for her, because after all, she was a useless sack of shit. And because her internal monologue was so self-hating, because her self-esteem was so low; she had a great need to find others upon whom she could transfer this well of self-loathing, be it a friend or just some stranger on the street. Her self-hatred gave her comfort, it filled up a void. Better a hive of negative voices than no voice; or more precisely, the voice of non-existence. Everyday felt like a ball and chain. Should Cindy just numb herself out with anti-depressants and live on a pink cloud? More like a pale beige cloud in her case; pink would be giving it too much credit. But then, anti-depressants were something that her mother was always suggesting, and there was no way was she going to do anything that her mother advised her to do. Cindy would purposely defy any positive suggestions coming from her progenitoresse; "consider the source", she rationalized ..... *I sure wish you would try those mood elevators honey. Who would want to be around you in your state of mind? If only you would just numb yourself out sexually, maybe then you could finally pass for dating material* ..... In terms of class, Cindy had the most in common with the Park Avenue Pearls and Blue Blazer-Type Bitches; whereas emotionally she had more in common with the toothless, mumbling bag lady with a shopping cart full of useless junk and a ratty old coat found in a dumpster that wasn't even good enough for the Salvation Army. *Quelle femme sans abri,* Cindy would murmur as she passed by this woman who looked like she had stuffed the lining of her coat with newspaper, who resembled something straight out of Hooverville. But Cindy Cipro would not bite the hand that fed her, that being the world of the Park Avenue Pearls and Blue Blazer-Type Bitches, with their disposable income and their ability to be autonomous and travel. They could take off for Paris or Rome or Madrid at the drop of a hat, even though they were usually too cheap to pay for first class, unless they "earned it" by means of their frequent flyer miles, which was as close to working as they would ever get. Besides the fact that their husbands had them on short leashes, so they would not overspend on clothes and jewelry. The Park Avenue Pearls and Blue Blazer-Type Bitches were parasites; they contrib- uted nothing to society, some had drinking and drug problems, some had children, and some had both.

The evening before, Cindy Cipro had actually fallen asleep exhausted, not because she had expended any effort manifesting her creativity; for example, getting to work on that steamy romance novel she had always wanted to write, that would have been a breeze for her given her backlog of thwarted fanta-sies. No, Cindy was exhausted because she had just spent six hours checking inside closets and behind all the furniture in her apartment for evil spirits, burglars, bogeymen and psychopathic serial sexual felons (six hours a day of checking made her, according to the latest statistics, severely obsessive-compulsive disor-dered). She checked for potential fires; she touched the wicks of candles hours after they had been extin-guished; she ran lit matches under water, and kept them there for as long a time as it took for her to real-ize that they were no longer flammable ..... ARE YOU FINALLY GONE NOW, FIRE ?!?!? ..... she would some-times scream in moments of panic. When she went on occasional smoking binges, she was afraid that the disposable lighters that she left on her coffee table would explode. She ran her fingers over the surface of all the electrical outlets; it was as if she had a special relationship with all the fixtures in her place, just as some people talk to plants, plants being some-thing she would never have in her apartment, not even flowers; she resented having to be responsible for anything but herself, particularly another living entity. Cindy Cipro could barely maintain her own wellbeing. She only wanted to destroy. Everything about the world outside the door of her womb-cave-prison was a threat. But tonight, she was worn out by her Inverse Discipline, and she fell asleep as soon as her head hit her loveless pillow.

And then the dreams began, the few that she could remember that is, which were always the high-light of her night ..... *Cindy was making desperate verbal attacks on everyone she came into contact with, pushing their buttons, pushing the envelope, until things began to get physical. She tightened silver screws into the temples of an army of goons who were out to get her. She slapped them silly, she ripped out their live and beating hearts, devouring the bloody organs ferociously, ignoring the latest FDA Standards .....* It was so much easier to meta-physically beat the shit out of everyone, instead of using that same energy to be calculating and clever, to play the game of life. *Life on life's terms!* Cindy snapped sarcastically, back in daytime reality. *That's what they always say at my Pal-Anon meeting. What a bunch of losers! If only they could follow their own*

advice! Then I might believe they were actually seri-
ous about self-improvement. She gathered the grain
from the silo of her bitterness, that bitterness that she
refused to ride through, to let wash over her like a
black wave. Why couldn't she just give in, release,
relax, be Zen, stop worrying, stop fighting so hard,
stop putting so much pressure on herself? Just make
friends with her demons instead of wishing they could
somehow be exorcised. To let go would have been
to finally know herself, to accept her limitations, to dis-
empower her negative preconceptions. What had
humankind, mankind, and womankind done to her
to make her so resentful? She couldn't imagine shar-
ing one positive, hopeful, unconditionally kind word
with anyone, now or ever. Her brain was on fire, and
flames were shooting out of her eyes, ears and mouth
like a fiery Gorgon-Dragon Fag Hag.

But tonight Cindy was having a subconscious
adventure that transcended all of her previous
dreams ..... *She was standing in a room looking at*
a long dining room table, impeccably set for the
upper class. The men were attired in white bow ties,
white shirts, white formal evening wear, and white

corsages. The table was covered with a white table-cloth, and was set with silver, crystal and fine white china. At each setting there were elaborately folded white cloth napkins. Three chandeliers lit the table from above at its beginning, middle and end points. All was symmetrical and beautiful. The guests were sipping red and white wine; they had attended a matinee at the opera that afternoon .....

Enter Cindy Cipro the Anarchic Force; all aris-tocracies have their eccentrics. Her name was on the guest list, she breezed in with a sense of entitle-ment that she could wear at will, even if she did not consider herself to the manor born. She wore black pearls, a black sleeveless linen dress, black heels, a black satin bow in her hair that gave her a high-end 1980's New Wave rebel look; her entire outfit was brand new, straight off the rack. She casually walked from one end of the table to the other. She courteously said "Excuse me" to a gentleman seated at one end of the table. Then she pulled the table-cloth towards her with superhuman force. The guests were startled as the glasses, dinnerware and can-delabras toppled; as the wine and the soup spilled.

as the entrees went flying off the plates. But no one stopped her. The tablecloth now lay on the floor in a heap. Cindy jumped up on the table, screaming and laughing; then she lay down on her side and started to roll herself from one end of the table to the other, soaking up all the various liquids that had combined to form a disgusting viscera, until her dress was saturated; she was maniacally ecstatic. She jumped off the table, picked up the sopping wet tablecloth from the floor, opened it up and began to pile the broken glass and dishes within its center. Once all the refuse had been piled onto the tablecloth, she tied it up like a sack, and began to beat that sack and its contents on the floor, still screaming and laughing. Once she had exhausted herself, she lay down her burden. Then she jumped up on the table yet again and pronounced: "This is my truth. I've shattered the props of your wasted, meaningless lives of indolence; what were formerly objects of luxury now represent the deformed ugliness of your grotesque hypocrisy. I bet you just had the best time of your lives, watching me defile myself in front of you. Wasn't it worth it? I had a blast!" And with that, she fell back off the *table and into her sack of refuse and passed out. The next thing she knew, she was waking up in her Houston Street apartment …..*

Cindy Cipro had been walking west on Houston Street. She had just passed the Landmark Sunshine Cinema, when she stopped at a crosswalk and noticed a fine-looking gentleman who was giving her the eye. Though by no means young, he wore his age well. This kind of situation, where someone was expressing interest in Cindy as "possible dating material" was guaranteed to freak her out. Anyone who cruised her was perceived as a threat. As she saw it, all romance led to tragedy, so why waste her time? So she yelled at this potential suitor: *Pruneface gets laid more than me. You hear me? Pruneface is getting all the action! I bet there's even some Pruneface with a pussy out there that'll give you what you want. In the meantime, I'm going home to give myself an enema; my intestines suddenly feel like an expanding balloon filled with boiling diarrhea! So now you know about my shit fetish. Too much information? Too bad! Good luck finding your next disposable fuck!* Said gentleman had of course scurried away well before Cindy had completed her misdirected diatribe. She knew it was a missed opportunity, but at that moment, she thought she was doing a favor to any person who potentially wanted to love her. She proceeded to her $975,000 one-bedroom apartment in the building above Unwholesome Broods, a steal in that neighborhood in those days, whose interior was decorated with various shades of gray. In spite of her constant state of misery, sometimes her Unbearable Heaviness of Being was a benefit; all of her myriad negative states would cancel each other out, and the clouds would part to reveal a silver lining, a gift. That gift appeared in the form of a message on her voice mail. Cindy had been invited to a New Year's Eve party that would take place on the next evening, on a Saturday .....

Whenever Cindy Cipro was able to tolerate a short-term affair, some guy would appear out of the blue, with whom she could debase herself. In that instance, her sexual adrenalin occupied the manic zone of her manic-depression. And so she had an affair with Fernando, and subsequently Carlos; they were both her type of alpha male, and took lovers of either sex easily. The two men traveled in similar circles, and in fact, despised each other; both were fiercely competitive. Eventually she found them in bed together, in a supreme expression of contemptuous lust, which was crushing, but at the same time, she liked it when it hurt so good. Evil portents had been hovering over her ever since her first date with Fernando, when he had told her point blank, *You're sick. You're a masochist. You like to suffer.* Secondly, since Cindy craved humiliation and degradation, that is what she got. *Be careful what you wish for!* her fair weather friends advised her (a fair-weather friend was the only kind of friend she knew). But Cindy went ahead and wished for it anyways; *I live in a world full of people who wish for what is bad for them; why should I be any different?* At Pal-Anon, she would share about how she had just gotten into another toxic relationship; her colleagues in recovery would roll their eyes. This reaction was not lost on Cindy, who would then close her eyes and pretend to meditate, while her fellow co-dependents would curse her in silence, or trash her later on at fellowship (Cindy called it *Fellow-Shit*), where vicious gossip was referred to as *the fourteenth step*. On the other hand, Cindy never believed the ones who tried to show her compassion; she could not take it in, because she did not believe that she had it to give back.

Cindy Cipro's unhappiness was caused by a simple lack of perspective. She never took the time to step back from the canvas of her life. Had she done so, she would have realized that she was seeking an explicit S & M scenario, in which both partners as consenting adults would follow a clear set of rules, thus allowing for the boundaries that Cindy so desperately needed. Encounters such as those would involve a safe word, both partners being aware that they were creating a scene, that was separate from whatever feelings they had for one another. Cindy had first met Fernando at one of those masked orgies frequented by jet setters, social climbers, and hustlers in the style of *Eyes Wide Shut* (although these parties were never as good as the one idealized by that film). It always seemed that the youthful, tanned, tattooed and six-packed men passed her over as damaged goods. But Cindy had gotten lucky at that particular orgy, where she had met Fernando; they hit it off well enough that they agreed to go back to her place. After their tryst of that first weekend, Fernando had left Cindy handcuffed to her wrought iron bedpost, and had told her that he was going out for coffee. She had entrusted him with the keys, and he showed up twenty-four hours later, barely faking his way through a "sorry", saying that he had forgotten about her being handcuffed (when in reality, he had gone to hook up with Carlos). Cindy had shat herself and pissed on the floor and she wore a raccoon mask created by running mascara (when she had first seen *Fatal Attraction*, her heart leapt! *That is the life I want!* she whispered to herself rapturously). Of course Cindy did not believe Fernando's excuse. Fernando unlocked the handcuffs and unsympathetically told her to clean up her mess and herself. And she liked this. Later on he sweet-talked her into believing that he cared about her, and Cindy pretended to believe him, as she could not face the prospect of creating any drama at that time; it was still too early in the relationship for the process of destruction to commence. Then Fernando was off to yet another tryst, this time with Hermana Morafin, an erotic adventurer with a chequered past. Fernando was a banker and he could pay for whatever he wanted. Hermana, being more wily and worldly than Cindy, was also having an affair with Carlos (unbeknownst to Fernando), since Fernando could not be depended upon. All of these various couplings maintained their intensity because they were secretive and transgressive.

And then there was Miguel, who was seeing both Carlos and Fernando; Miguel had no interest in women, and referred to himself as a *faggy fag*. To the uninformed eye, it would seem that Fernando was the winner among Hermana, Miguel and Cindy, being that he was able to successfully juggle three simultaneous affairs. But whatever pleasure Fernando derived from these situations was counteracted by the stress resulting from living such a compartmentalized life, which was undermining his sanity. Seven weeks after Miguel had begun his affairs with both Fernando and Carlos, Miguel was murdered. His body was found washed up on the shore of the East River with his arms and legs cut off in the manner of *Boxing Helena* (ironically, that had been one of Miguel's favorite films). Miguel had had few friends, as well as a distant, dysfunctional family; according to that logic, it was no surprise that he had fallen through the cracks. Was this simply a case of Inverse Creative Visualization? Or had Miguel subconsciously willed himself off the Blue Green Planet? As for Fernando and Carlos, who knows what was going through their minds. It was highly probable that one of them had been involved in Miguel's murder.

One day, Cindy Cipro noticed an article in the New York Post about Miguel's death; the killer was still at large. Intuitively, she found this incident to be highly disturbing. having no idea that both Fernando had been involved with Miguel. Fernando, as well as Carlos, had always met Miguel in a sauna or sex club, never at Miguel's place. This cloak of anonymity provided both Fernando and Carlos with alibis. There was no such thing as a lonely night in the lives of either one of them; nights spent watching television, surfing the Internet, reading a book, overeating, or contemplating suicide. Fernando and Carlos were both men of action; existentialists. Life was short and they were going to make the best of it .....

The New Year's Eve party took place in a chic House Beautiful kind of loft on Bowery between Prince and Spring Streets, that was decorated in muted earth colors; beige, tan, pale yellow, faded brick red, silver, gray and white. Cindy was drinking her glass of bordeaux slowly, waiting for the right moment to strike. It wouldn't be long now; half of the guests were already comfortably drunk; the party had begun around nine. Cindy had arrived shortly after midnight to avoid the New Year's countdown and subsequent smooch fest. Fernando was there, as well as Carlos; she ignored Fernando. Carlos paid her no mind; he was used to her moodiness. At one in the morning, securely ensconced in a luxurious slate gray armchair, Cindy made her pronouncement. There was no need to introduce herself, she just started enunciating loudly with a big sarcastic smile on her face .....

"ATTENTION! ATTENTION! THIS IS GOING TO BE SHORT AND NOT AT ALL SWEET! I THINK EVERYONE OF YOU HERE IS A FAKE, A PHONY, A HUSTLER, A KOONT, A SLOOT, A KRACKHÜR, A SOCIOPATH, A NARCISSIST, A MEGALOMANIAC, A PATHOLOGICAL LIAR. JUST IN

CASE I MISSED ANYONE, JUST IN CASE ANYONE FEELS LEFT OUT: THAT INCLUDES THE DRUGGIES, THE FAGS, THE FAG HAGS, THE FETISHISTS, THE GEEKS, THE NERDS, THE DRUIDYCK-WYCKAN-PAGANS, THE QUEENS, THE QUEERS, THE TRANSVESTITES, THE TRANSSEXUALS, THE TRANSGENDERS, THE WIMPS, THE WEIRDOES, AND LAST BUT NOT LEAST—MY FAVORITE--THE WALLFLOW-ERS! ALL OF YOU--GO FUCK YOURSELVES! I HAVE NOTHING TO LOSE! GO AHEAD--BE DEFENSIVE! LET US START SOME SHIT! NO ONE IS EVER GOING TO TELL YOU LIKE IT IS, LIKE I HAVE DONE IN THIS SCINTILLATING MOMENT!"

At first, there was silence and consternation among the guests after Cindy's oration. Some of the partygoers had looks on their faces that said, *Who the fuck is that and why has she so boldly told us off?* Then, one by one, the guests, mostly Euro trash drinking champagne, smoking, smirking, wearing party hats, secure in their secular lives of indulgence, began to stare at her malevolently. Cindy stood there and watched them, trying to appear unmoved, but there was no question; she was feeling regretful for what she had said, and she was afraid.

This was not the response she had expected. She had thought that everyone would have just laughed at her; maybe they would have even hurt her feelings, yet leave her stronger for enduring that which would not kill her. So Cindy Cipro moved on to Plan B. She jumped onto the back of the woman she had identified as the female alpha whore, whom she envied above all, and began scratching, gouging, kicking, pummeling, and pounding her. Upon witnessing this, Fernando, who was definitely seeing Cindy in a new light, shouted to the group: *She is our captive now. I'm going for the cutlery ….. Take your time.* *We'll pin her down*, shouted back two other guests, a couple of performance artists who went by the names of Princess Orca Media and Genevieve Piss Pig. Fernando returned with the cutlery, as well as every type of kitchen utensil he could find--he had even run across a toolbox--and distributed the weapons. Then the group fell upon Cindy with knives, forks, potato mashers, corkscrews and soup ladles. They pulled back each of Cindy's fingers until the bones snapped. They speared the backs of her hands with forks. Princess Orca Media and Genevieve Piss Pig used hammers to pound on Cindy's fingernails, one by one. They hammered the backs of her hands, cracking the bones. Cindy's toes were then smashed with hammers, and the tops of Cindy's feet were gouged with screwdrivers. As Cindy retreated into a zone between shock and unconsciousness, she mumbled to herself, *I should have thrown myself from the mezzanine balcony after the first act of "Wycked"*. Then Carlos shouted into Cindy's face: *Happy New Year! Enjoy it while you last!* Then one resourceful guest, who had boiled some water in an electric teakettle, poured it onto Cindy's face. Then corkscrews were jammed into Cindy's skull. Then Fernando checked to make sure everyone present had his or her party hats on, and counted down: *Three--Two--One!* Then the group blew their noisemakers and sang, *Happy Death Day to You!* in unison. As the *pièce de resistance,* they smashed Cindy's face in with a marble rolling pin.

Unfortunately, Cindy Cipro had expired before they had finished the first verse of *Happy Death Day to You!* They were having so much fun that they did not even notice her final death throes. This was a big disappointment; they had underestimated how much they would actually enjoy killing her, and they were sorry that the process could not have gone on longer. Cindy had deliberately provoked the group into giving her what they thought she had wanted; that her life be ended. When the time came around, Cindy's family would not even investigate the reasons for her murder. They had assumed that she had fallen in with a bad crowd. But then, her family had bought her off, and thus disposed of her years ago, like a broken doll that one nonchalantly tosses into a pile of junk in the attic.

Due to their class differences, two girls who would otherwise never have known each other, would receive that opportunity. Cindy Cipro would now be joining Alison "One L" Shitbox on the faux Oral Roberts University campus of the Watchtower Paradise Afterlife .....

PRINCESS ORCA MEDIA

    Princess Orca Media bathed herself in high-end medieval soaps, doused herself with perfumes and tried to forget about the smells of manure that often wafted up to the windows of the castle tower, as she luxuriated in her secluded chamber, drawing comfort from the flickering of candlelight upon her surroundings of polished stone. Imports of whatever product she desired, that would make her life easier than ninety nine percent of the peasant rabble that constituted the demographic of her queendom, could be obtained with a simple command. The Christian Knights Templar brought her essential oils of lavender, rose, and verbena; finely ground cedar and juniper berries; pine needles crushed and then stuffed into aromatic pillows; morning glory seeds to be ingested for what would become known as a type of acid trip hundreds of years later. And rosemary; she was passionate about rosemary. She would boil it with jasmine green tea, transported back from the Orient. She steeped together chamomile, thyme, and garlic, which she would then consume as a healthful broth. Sacks of rose petals were brought to her, to be boiled in a cauldron, creating a potpourri whose fragrance transfixed her. And when all this was done, she would take the stewed remains of the herbs and flowers, steep them with lemon rinds, drain this mixture and use it as a compost for the royal garden. Her quarters functioned as a laboratory of aromatherapy. [Although most of the populace, especially those outside the castle walls, died before the age of forty; during this era there existed a knowledge of herbology and a connection to the earth and nature that would eventually vanish in the over-sanitized conditions of the far-distant twenty-first century.] These were the perks of royalty; of the spoiled, demanding, pre-Freudian and power-drunk bitches of her time. If Princess Orca Media's temper became too heated and she was deemed to be potentially threatening to her Handmädchens, especially during her frequent morning glory trips, the priest of the court would be called upon to perform an exorcism.

Orca Media drank in the warmth of the crackling flames emanating from the gigantic stone fireplace, as she was buffed dry by her Handmädchens with towels made from Egyptian cotton. The castle walls were thirty feet thick and a drawbridge crossed over a deep moat; ever watchful guards protected her from everyday dangers suffered by her subjects with their much shorter life spans. Just beyond the moat, Orca Media's people engaged in lusty, dirty battle; ever ready to die as heroes for causes they had always believed to be noble. The Princess ruled over these wastrels condescendingly, with a lack of compassion typical of extreme narcissists. But Orca Media could not intimidate them; she could not stamp out their fire. Much of the serfs' resentment was due to the fact that feasts awaited the Princess nightly; repasts comprised of the diet of the upper echelon of the medieval world. At these feasts, the lords and ladies of the court enjoyed viande, game, cheeses, grapes, wines, and whatever fruits and vegetables were available in a given season. All of this abun-dance was too much for even Orca Media herself. On many occasions, after the completion of yet another sumptuous smorgasbord embellished with jewel-encrusted goblets and candlesticks, she fled to the horses' stable to vomit into their manure buckets. Since anorexia nervosa and bulimia were unknown at the time, Orca Media's Handmädchens created a cover story for her royal peers, so as not to raise suspi-cion as to the true nature of her physical and mental condition that remained undiagnosed.

And since there was no television, classes both high and low enjoyed Sunday mass in the smoky frankincense-filled cathedral, that perfume disguis-ing the squalid odors of the local populace who were clothed in malodorous rags. The Princess took delight in these services as a respite from her queenly calendar. Her presence was required in most cases, whether she liked it or not, whatever her personal beliefs were; she played the role of one of the faithful to still any would-be-grumbling from the unruly mob, who were ever ready to label her an elitist. Out-side of the cathedral, superstition and acts of God influenced the whims of the peasant horde; a solar eclipse could inspire either rash violence or benign indifference. There were many nights when Princess Orca Media remained wide awake with a pain in her chest, convinced that she would be stabbed or strangled before dawn. then heaved out of the tower window, crashing onto the rocks of various preci-pices before landing lifeless in the moat. Recently subjects of a lower station, who had started to feel suffocated and unappreciated, had snapped and became killers, although few of them got away with murder, thanks to the practice of vigilante justice that prevailed in the court.

One night, Princess Orca Media had a dream from the future. She was addressed by a faceless voice, in a language that she did not understand, from a land that she did not recognize. She needed a release from the psychic stress of a life where on the one hand, she was completely responsible, but on the other hand, she was entirely bored …..

"FUCK YOU RAPUNZEL SAINT PFANNQUEQUE, YOU THINK YOU'RE ALL THAT UP IN YOUR TOWER WITH YOUR BLONDIE GIRLIE TRESSES HANGING DOWN, WHAT'S

IT LIKE UP THERE WITH ALL YOUR MONEY, PERFUME AND PRETTY THINGS, YOU FEEL PRETTY?!?! WHAT'S IT LIKE DOING NOTHING BUT LISTENING TO BIRIDIES SING ON COOL SPRING DAYS WITH BLUE SKIES AND WHITE PUFFY CLOUDS?!?! WHAT HAPPENS WHEN IT RAINS?!?! I BET YOU ARE THE BITCH OF SOMEBODY, YOU PLAY THE INNOCENT, BUT YOU ARE REALLY THE BEAST, OR THE VICTIM OF SOME MONSTER, OR A MONSTER YOURSELF?!?! WATCH OUT, I'M GOING TO COME UP THERE WITH MY HOMIES, WITH MY HOWZIES, WITH MY MAISONIES, "NOUS VENONS CHEZ TOI, WIR KOMMEN NACH HAUSE, UM DICH ZU HAUSE ZU SEHEN!!!!" DO YOU MIND IF I ASK YOU SOME PERSONAL QUESTIONS?!?!? WHO IS YOUR MAN?!?! DO YOU HAVE ONE?!?! OR IS YOUR IVORIE TOWER YOUR PHALLICK SUBSTITUTE, SINCE NO MAN IS GOOD ENOUGH FOR YOU?!!?! CAREFUL HOW YOU PLAY OR YOU'LL END UP LIKE DJZHEEMI SPARKS, HE LIVES IN AN IVORIE TOWER TOO!!!! HE'S A DRUIDYCK-WYCKAN-PAGAN QUEER-FAGGOT-SCREAMER!!! ER IST DAS BITCH!!!! I WILL BE WATCHING YOU!!!! I WORSHIP GÜTRÜNE NEUSCHWAN-STEIN, JUST LIKE DZHJEEMI, SHE'S MORE POWERFUL THAN THE HAWK-HEADED GODDDESS, MAYA HIYUH

POWUH, OR EVEN LORD SZCZMAWG!!!! ACCEPT ME AS YOUR DOMINANT VOICE, GIVE ALL YOUR POWER AWAY TO ME, RAPUNZEL SAINT PFANNQUEQUE, YOU CAN'T DESTROY ME, MY ESSENCE RESIDES IN ALL YOUR CHILDHOOD TOYS, YOUR CANDYLAND, YOUR EASY BAKE OVEN, YOUR ETCH-A-SKETCH!!!! I AM HAUNTING EBAY!!! I JUST WANTED TO DROP BY AND SAY HI, TO CATCH UP, TO TOUCH BASE, TO WISH YOU WELL; ALL THE BEST, BITCH!!!! NEVER FORGET HOW EVIL I AM!!! I MAKE 'INLAND EMPIRE' LOOK LIKE THE SEVEN HILLS GIRL SCOUT CAMP OF YOUR KINDHEIT!!!! GOOD LUCK WITH ALL YOUR PROJECTS, EVERYONE THINKS YOU'RE SO TALENTED, BETTER GET THOSE NEW HEADSHOTS MISS LAZY, THERE'S SOME UNDERGRADUATE AT COLUMBIA UNIVERSITY WHO WANTS TO CAST YOU IN A STUDENT FILM; YOU'D BE PERFECT AS THE LOBOTOMIZED WHORE WHOSE COMBINED SAT SCORES WERE MINUS FIFTY!!!! SO LONG FOR NOW, RAPUNZEL SAINT PFANNQUEQUE!!! MORE THAN ANYTHING, I WANT YOU TO TAP INTO YOUR SOURCE, TO BECOME THE HIGHEST VERSION OF YOUR-SELF! I WANT EVERYONE I KNOW TO BE THE BEST THEY CAN BE!!!" Then the voice faded away as if it was being sucked down into a whirlpool .....

The next day, a German envoy from what is present day Niedersachsen arrived to meet Princess Orca Media's handlers in the Main Hall of the castle, to discuss a possible transaction of marriage to Prince Engelbert Alles Nicht Egal. Orca Media considered Engelbert to be a good catch, as he was easy on the eyes. Even if this relationship ended up being not particularly deep, meaningful or soulful; still, the Princess could expect more than just having to lie in a rigid missionary position while Engelbert grunted on top of her, that kind of situation being the status quo of the arranged political alliances of those times. Orca Media summoned one of her Handmädchens and bade her to spy on Prince Engelbert's orientation; although this Handmädchen risked execution for being caught spying, she also risked being beheaded for disobeying the Princess' orders. And so Orca Media informed her Handmädchen: *Keep thyself occulted behind the plush Tyrrhenian purple curtains, their density shall muffle any escape of breath that shall arise from thy person. But before doing so, fetch my clean undergarments that hath been pressed and pounded with rocks and soaked in the cold mountain stream to eradicate any traces of liquids from my orifices .....*

REMEMBER HOW IT IS COMMONLY SAID .....

THE DIRTIEST FANTASIES HAPPEN IN THE CLEANEST BEDS .....

My inner vixen shall surface from the depths and my feminine wiles shall triumph. Listen with a keen ear and report any suspicions that thou findest to be troubling back to me anon, once our Teutonic envoy's orientation hath adjourned. And see that my German language counselour be made ready, so I can benefit from his lessons therewith .....

Indeed, Princess Orca Media's German had progressed to an intermediate level, due to diligent practice that she had achieved with her servants. *Was ist denn los, Krackhüren der tiefen Nacht? Bald muß ich Kama Sutra mit dem Engelbert Alles Nicht Egal machen .....* Her Handmädchens understood not one word she uttered, but they nodded their heads quaintly, trying to suppress their barely-contained terror by offering fragile, conciliatory smiles.

Orca Media's jokes did not make any sense in German, but she was not enthusiastic about learning foreign tongues, the study of which was merely a practical necessity of that era. And so she satirized the entire process, at least in her own mind, with a sense of humour that was lost on all of her courtly handlers.

Then Girl from Future teleported herself into the Princess' chamber .....

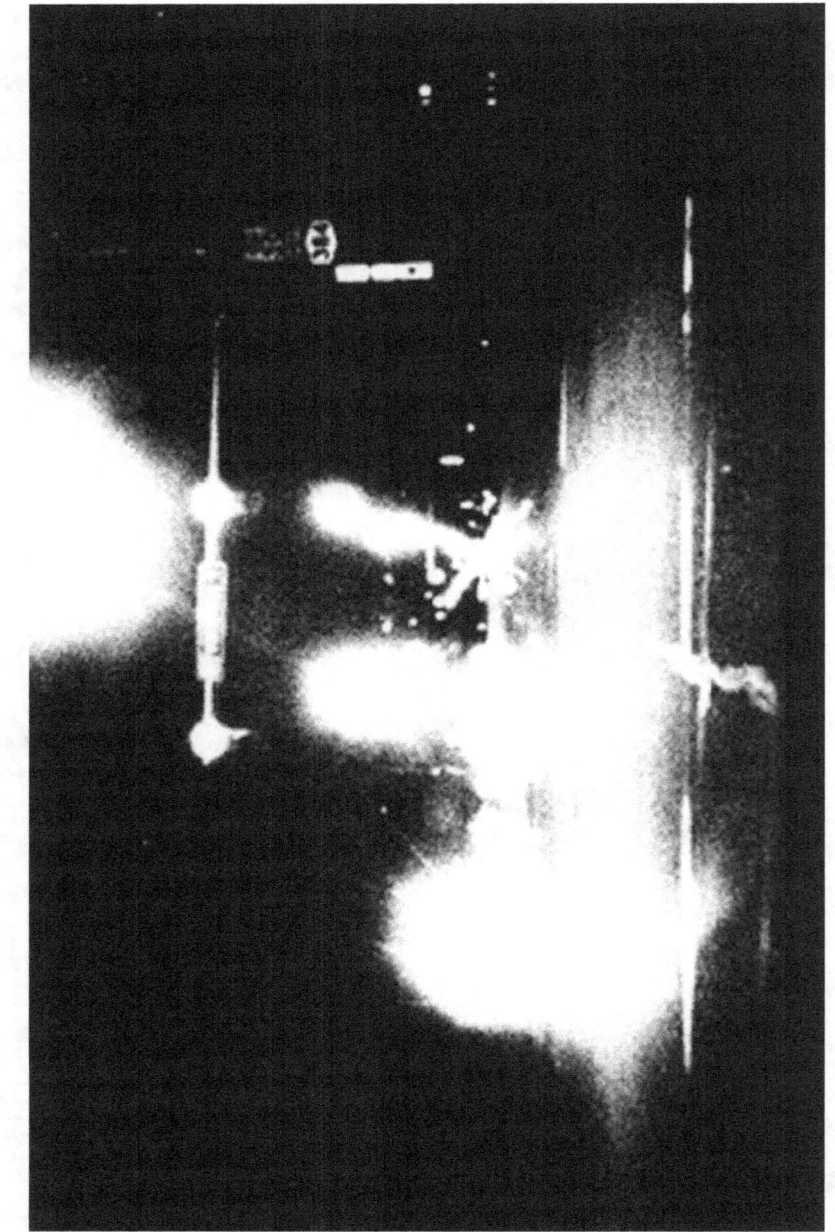

GIRL FROM FUTURE

When Girl from Future appeared, she was wearing black patent leather pumps with taps on their
heels, black fishnet stockings, a black patent leather
bustier, a custom-made black wig with bangs in the
style of Louise Brooks, black lipstick, nails done with
black nail polish; her alabaster cheeks powdered
extravagantly with purple rouge. She wore silver rings
on her fingers and silver bracelets on her wrists. She
had also brought along a Hula Hoop and a Frisbee
to be unpredictably camp, because she was more
than just an intimidating Burlesque Goth Girl. She was
a businesswoman for whom every hour of the day
was scheduled ahead of time. And since she was
also ahead of her time, even in her own time, the
twenty-first century, she had decided to return to the

Middle Ages to give herself an even greater superiority complex. Girl from Future had beamed into Princess Orca Media's quarters via Backward Time Teleportation, and she could return to the future at her leisure by means of a Porn Key provided to her by her Sexually Ambiguous Life Coach, Genevieve Piss Pig. The Princess was shocked by Girl from Future. Once Orca Media had calmed herself, she managed to say ..... *How comest thou and thy deportments here? Beest thou a celestial vision? What are these strange garments adorning thy vampirically pale flesh? What manner of conveyance hath deposited thee into the interior of my highly guarded and fortified castle?*

Girl from Future answered in her Joisey accent ..... *I took the Wormhole from Cape Canaveral with this Porn Key. You know about Backward Time Teleportation? With this Porn Key, I can go wherever the fuck I want; any place, any time! My atoms were rearranged and recombined with dilithium crystals, like the transporter did in Star Trek? And I mean the original 1966-1969 classic series; do you know what I'm saying? Except instead of beaming down, I beamed* back! I don't know how the fuck it works; I ain't no fuckin' rocket scientist!

I know you won't understand what I'm talking about, but I love Florida! It's cheap to live there; you get a lot of space for not much money. So what if the water bugs are the size of rats! I sell weed; I hate nine to five. So here I am, and well; maybe we can party? I heard there's this new drug made with bath salts? How about we mix it up with some coke, crystal meth, or oxycontin; I'm open to experimentation! I mean, look at me! Judging from your outfit, I can see that you people dress really different; one of the great advantages of time travel is the chance to see new things! I could see you on one of those historical public television shows where the narrators have super-polite British accents. Really, you look far out! Oh Maya Hiyuh Powuh, I love that old Star Trek! I even thought Captain Kirk was pretty foxy back in the day! And what a player, huh? Always putting the moves on some strange Endorian femme fatale with blue hair! Besides running a spaceship, he was getting a lot of snatch! (I would never let any guy, or girl for that matter, call my vagina a snatch, even though I use that word to describe other women all the time). Back to Captain Kirk: what a multi-tasker, what a compartmentalizer! I mean, I loved The Twilight Zone too, but it scared the shit out of me! I wonder why ..... was it the paranoid Cold War symbolism? I read once in the Village Voice that the 1964 "Rudolph the Red-Nosed Reindeer" Christmas special was a metaphor for the evil workings of the Soviet Union! Wow, was I naïve back then! I was still sucking my thumb when I was fifteen. I used to beat myself up about that, but I found out years later that certain friends of mine were still sucking their thumbs when they were 35! In high school, I couldn't get to sleep on the nights before gym days. That's how freaked out I was! Isn't it ridiculous, all the petty shit you worry about? Then one day you wake up and realize that you're going to die, that no-one gives a fuck about you, and that you better start trying to make your mark before the Grim Reaper cuts you down! I know what you're thinking ..... C'mon say it! You think I'm getting too old for this outfit, right?

Plus, my parents were always ignoring me! So I retreated into a fantasy world, and ever since then *life has been so disappointing! I mean, I'm making the best of it, and I'm not a downer! I have coping skills; I front with my Bitch-Whore-Koont-Sloot persona! I'm not special! Everyone's putting on an act, everyone's a phony! Fuck you world! At the same time, you've got to be careful about who you tell off. My friend Cindy Cipro, this dumb snatch I used to know with too much time and money on her hands (no disrespect intended); she trashed everyone she knew to their face, and ended up being murdered! She took everything the wrong way! As punishment, she'll now be spending an eternity with Alison "One L" Shitbox on the faux Oral Roberts University campus of the Watchtower Paradise Afterlife. Thanks be to the Hawk Headed Goddess that I'm so different from how Cindy was! I'm tough! Even if I like those kind of guys that are like, "Okay honey, I fucked you, so get the fuck out, cuz I have to get ready for the next bitch that's comin' over!" I can deal with that! When those player types piss me off, I just threaten to cut off their schlongs with an Eckzackto knife, until they scram ..... !*

Princess Orca Media just stood there, astonished, hypnotized, uncomprehending. Girl from Future continued:

Are you bored, Princess? Are we on the same wavelength? Do you understand Amurycka Profundan English? What country am I in? What are you, German or something? "Auf Deutsch, bitte?" Hey, I know this joke in German, check this out: "Hallo, ich heiße Kandie Von Krackhüren!" Well it's not a joke exactly; it's just a funny thing I say! "Candy the Crackwhore!" It's the same thing in English! Am I in Burgundie? Would you happen to have a jug of Gallow burgundie on you? Time travel makes me so thirsty! Even lambruszczko would be okay ..... Or Szczill a Szczella; remember Szczill a Szczella?!?! Mawteenie and Rawszczie on the Rawkkszcz?!?! Kamparie can be very refreshing with a slice of lime! I'm sorry, but I'm not one of those elegant Shakespearean speaking dames! What's wrong? Why are your eyeballs going back up inside of your head? How many kinds of anti-depressants are you on? Are you in therapy? Wait a minute; from the looks of this place, psychoanalysis hasn't even been invented yet!

900 Years Later

Princess Orca Media has been reincarnated as a crass, reality television-style chick from Joisey, who is trying to tighten up her A-list material at comedy clubs in the Tri-State area. She even lands a gig now and then at clubs up and down the Eastern seaboard. Girl from Future had gone back in time to visit her, to give her a glimpse of that upcoming life. But Orca Media had been unable to grasp the essence of that event. The Princess had suppressed all conscious awareness of her past incarnations as well.

GENEVIEVE PISS PIG

Before moving onto her next life, Princess Orca Media had opened a Door to the Future, using a piece of chalk to demarcate the boundaries of the Portal to Forward Time Teleportation on a thick stone wall, in the manner of *Laberinto de la Fauna*. That Door to the Future opened onto a passageway, leading to Klub Nicht-So-Geil in Berlin, Doucheyland. At the end of that passageway was Genevieve Piss Pig, laughing hysterically and violently like a younger version of Martha from *Who's Afraid of Virginia Woolf*. "I LOVE THESE TUNNELS OF TIME TELEPORTATION", she said. "THEY REMIND ME OF WIDE OPEN ASSHOLES THAT HAVE BEEN PREPARED FOR COLONOSCOPIES!" Genevieve was surrounded by a sparkling, crackling light, and was dressed in nineteen-eighties Goth-

Punk-Space Age-Motorcycle attire; her look combined the best aspects of Siouxsie Sioux and Mad Max. "Don't be intimidated by my aggressive yet ebullient nature", intoned Genevieve. "In my Introvert World, I'm like Häley Comet Mills in *The Kaukäzian Chalk Garden Familie Circle*, or anything else she starred in, in which she was always delightful and sweet. I too, am the Pollyanna! Or I resemble my friend Djzheemi Sparks! Djzheemi the Inimitable! Djzheemi the Infamous! Djzheemi, we hardly knew ye!" And with that, Genevieve fell into a reminiscence .....

We met in New York City. Djzheemi went to all the darkrooms and backrooms in New York, and eventually on every continent on the Blue Green Planet! He was not the rainbow-flag waving, lavender-loving, photo op with one thousand of his best friends at the circuit party type! No, he was the exact opposite of that. He used to brag about this connection he had to the Great Chain of Being; to the Surrealists and to the Beatniks; "Back when there were real artists!" he would proclaim proudly, as if he was Alfred Jarry. He liked to think of himself as an artist / intellectual / Ren-

aissance man, but his sensibility was closer to that of a hacky road comic.

Djzheemi couldn't even make a living at that, because he spent all his time in his Ivorie Tower writing essays and treatises that would never see the light of day! Sure, he would submit his work to the industry to try and gain recognition, but he handled rejection so poorly that he gave up and decided to become a hedonist. And he failed at that as well! So many bad choices he made! Here was a really driven guy, who didn't know what the fuck he wanted! Here is a description of his work ethic: procrastination, confusion, insecurity, laziness, doubt, paranoia, fear of exposure. He mistrusted and disrespected everyone he came into contact with! And in spite of everything negative I've said about him, I still thought he could make something of himself.

Then he met up with Günther Glückwünsch; Djzheemi always needed to have a shady, disreputable type in the outer orbit of his friendships; that was his Achilles' high heel. Günther introduced him to European decadence; in other words: sex without shame! Günther tried to help him get over his puritanism; he took him to nude beaches and orgies in Ibiza. But Djzheemi needed his puritanism, he depended upon it, he needed to rebel against it, in order to be an artist. I kept telling him, "Djzheemi, artists work, they produce, they make things; in the end, it's not so different from the nine to five world you scoff at!" He ended up as a mindless, faceless night tripping Dionysian, though the Ibizans howled with laughter at his pale skin and his prudish manner .....

One day, shortly before the end, I ran into him in the East Village; he was completely plastered and high on who knows what kind of toxic combination of drugs. And he said to me, slurring his words, "I just want to enjoy life, man!" Those words came back to haunt me. In high school, even though Djzheemi was thought by many to be an eccentric, they recognized that he had talent and that he would go places. But twenty years after he had graduated from high school, he was still going to open mikes, and writing a blog that no one ever read! He was a Sunday painter every day of the week! Of course there are no guarantees that anyone will achieve success; we don't even know if we'll be here tomorrow! Excuse me for sounding fatalistic, but I think F. Scott Fitzgerald was right when he said: "There are no second acts in American lives ....."

Genevieve stopped; looked down, regained her composure and then continued. "But enough about Djzheemi! Djzheemi's dead! And in spite of that I still can't forgive him for draining me and for using me! Nietzsche was right; the artist is a vampire! Did Nietzsche say that? I'm not sure, don't quote me; I'm not a quasi-intellectual dilettante like Djzheemi was. How dare I speak ill of the dead! Who am I to judge? My own life has been reprehensible as well. I spend a lot of time on my knees in the half-light of semi-gray or even pitch-black dark rooms. Name a continent, besides Greenland, and I'll find a back room there! By the way, if you happen to see me in one of those decadent *milieux* looking dejected, this does not mean I'm unhappy. It's all part of my image-manip-ulation technique to render myself more attractive, even in the role of sexual servant / doormat. And I'm talking doormat by design; I'm no victim! I convert passivity into passion, and victimhood into victory! Who doesn't know that the more you hate yourself, the more attractive you become! Well, at least on a short-term basis .....

On my final Walk of Schäme, I'll spontaneously combust and provide the dying Blue Green Planet with more energy than a quarter gram of anti-matter. [Yes, I read *Faggots and Screamers*, the first book in Fan Crown's series before *Da Bitchy Koont*; I'm not so elitist that I can't enjoy a best seller.] And after I am pulverized, I will rematerialize like the phoenix. [Which mind you, is nothing like the derivative phoenix of Kallous Humblewhore in Che Mary Kay Foul-Thyng's *'Higher Parterre'* series]. I mean a phoenix, as it was originally defined, in the context of classical Greek mythology, and all of its ancestral mythologies .....

I've failed at pretending to be German. It didn't take them long to expose me, as I mangled and desecrated their baroque and highly structured language. Whorey Roboman Empire hypocrites! *Hier ist die Wahrheit:* I'm not brave enough to be an exhibitionist in a fully lit space and not brash enough to pretend to be a Joisey-style pole dancer like Maryszcza Tomato in *Duh Wreszczlur*. Even though the Berliners have exposed me as a fake not worthy of their advanced fetishistic practices, I am willing to forgive, as I am transsexual-fixed by their wonderfully piney smelling dishwashing detergents. *Ja, die Umwelt ist sehr wichtig! Bitte, Schnell und Sauber, gnädige Frau!* Those Germans are not so kalt-hearted as the Amurycka Profundans have been taught to believe. They have a tradition of deep thinking: *Die Philsophie, Der Sozialismus, Der Kommunismus, Der Rassismus, Der Pessimismus ….. Hier ist meine Phantasie:"*

Genevieve Piss Pig peers around a corner and into the Chamber of Urinals, where she is being observed peripherally by those lost to oblivion. Although women rarely participate in the gatherings of this used-to-be-secret society, they are not necessarily shunned. Ugly sexy Germano-Slavic men of various body types sit in the corners of the bathroom of Klub Nicht-So-Geil, on either side of five urinals lined up side by side on the wall, waiting to drink the piss of the men standing at those urinals. Those men in the corners even want their clothes, waterproofed or not, to be saturated with urine. Their brutish, bestial faces make them very appealing, a *Willkommen* change from the tan, tattooed, six-packed disco faeries who appear on the covers of slick LGBT literature, like SEXT Magazine, to market myriad products suitable for an idealized version of decadent gay life. *Zum Beispiel:* "Klamydya Karnyval Kroozes": at each stop on the tour, the boys have yet another chance to pick up a case of antibiotic-resistant gonorrhea!

One of those passive piss-fetishists is lying down on his back in the urinal chamber, his latest captor having placed his black-booted foot on the neck of his victim. The captor is yet another exaggerated neo-punk pseudo-motorcyclist sporting black vulcanized rubber space age gear. It is unclear whether the passive is truly consenting and enjoying this abuse, but the aggressor is obviously relishing his moment of power. Tomorrow will be another story however, as the two of them have tickets to see *Die Dreigro-schenoper* at the *Stadtoperhaus,* a black-tie event where everyone will be looking spiffy, gleaming, well groomed, manicured, perfumed, waxed, buffed.

Out in the dark room foyer-gossip chamber, numerous fetishists, who don't necessarily look so great in their outfits, smoke cigars and cigarettes until the smoke becomes so thick as to diminish any kind of aphrodisiac ambiance. These men are never as tough as they look, but their quasi-moody visages heighten the erotic potential of the moment. Some of these fetishists are wearing gas masks; it's not that they're bothered by the smoke; on the contrary, it's all about the look …..

Genevieve Piss Pig proceeds to give head to a naked man writhing in a cage as he sniffs poppers while smiling lewdly and making lascivious pelvic gestures. She remains on the outside looking in, her mouth inserted between two bars of the cage. After the Writhing Man ejaculates onto the floor, he loses interest in her. *Haben Sie keine Pisse für mich?* she asks. But the Writhing Man just laughs at her as if he was Jeanne Moreau in *Querelle*. Genevieve starts to rattle the bars of the cage in frustration. She will have to calm down, because anger never goes over well in these dungeons of depravity.

Genevieve Piss Pig has had enough; no sense in pushing fun. There will be plenty to be had another time should she be in the mood. The smell of cigars and cigarettes has become oppressive, the sinks are clogged and the rubbish receptacles are overflowing with brown paper towels. This is the antithesis of the spic and span daytime *Berliner* world in which white, green and brown glass is deposited for recycling purposes into individual white, green and brown mound-shaped containers that frequently appear along the sidewalks of the city.

A wiry young Moroccan man comes buzzing into the club like a yellow jacket. If he is not high on crack, then he is hyped up on something very similar *(wahrscheinlich ist er ein Krackhür)*. He gesticulates constantly and makes grotesque, comic faces. He speaks several languages: German, Arabic, French, Spanish, and of course English. His appearance in Klub Nicht-So-Geil is a sign to the *Ledermänner*, should they desire to return to a semblance of daytime reality, that the early-morning shift has begun and it is time for the less conventional, or less desperate, to leave.

And so Genevieve feels compelled to depart as well. The presence of the Moroccan Krackhür Harlequin Hustler is always a bad omen. She steps out into the gray morning light and feels free. She has no intention of making this a Walk of Schäme. Everyone

in the club had begun to look ghoulish; they resembled George Grosz' portraits of bourgeois men as
Schweine. As she walks along the street that will take
her to the main venue of the *Bermuderdreieck*, she
says a prayer to Lord Szczmawg, thanking him for the
opportunity to continue to breathe *die frische Luft* of
the Blue Green Planet. Then Genevieve Piss Pig stops
in front of Klub Djzhaxx. whirls a Porn Key around her
head seven times, and vanishes into a Portal of Backward Time Teleportation.

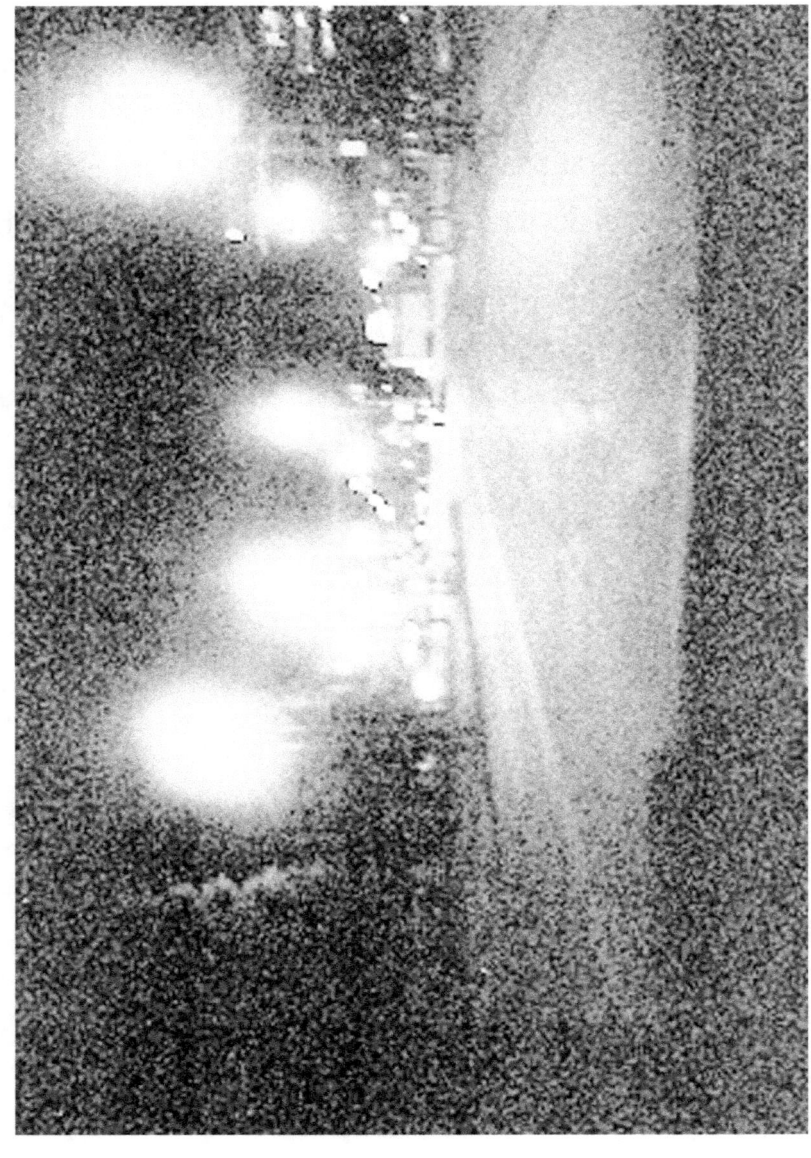

ALLISON ECKSLACKS WELLNESS

Allison Eckslacks Wellness had always loved the world portrayed in *Jules et Jim*; a place that titillated her fantasies of living a life she was afraid to even imagine, so forbidden had that kind of thinking been by her elders. When she allowed herself, she pictured herself participating in a *ménage à trois* with two other men, and while neither of them were always available, that was the price one paid for that genre of relationship. The fact is, she was mentally unstable, unpredictable, unhinged. If she was going to live her life in a chalet in the Alps, surrounded by fields of buttercups, daisies and edelweiss, in a place where she could finally call the shots, she was going to have to learn how to relax. And so Allison entertained this fantasy on a cool day in April, as she sat at the kitchen table in West Whoreland, Faerie County, New York, looking out the window at the swampy field, over-grown with the beautiful but aggressively invasive Purple Loosestrife, Queen Anne's Lace, Black-Eyed Susans and the occasional tree. Life was good, she thought.

Allison had been born in West Whoreland, and planned on spending the rest of her life there. Her happiness was unrelated to her being defined by a male partner; unrelated to her being a purposeful contributor to the community of fine upstanding citizens of which she was a part; unrelated to that part of herself that always tried to be so good. Although she did not participate in any organized religion, she was spiritual; she believed in karma, reincarnation, mindfulness, shamanism and other once exotic concepts that had gradually crept into the mainstream values of her politically mixed township. She drifted off into a NIGHT + NIGHT = DOUBLE DARK = DOUBLE BLACK dream .....

Now Allison Eckslacks Wellness was in Middle Earf Hampton for the quiet time after Anti-Labour Day weekend. She was blissfully unaware as she performed scathing, balletic synchronized swimming-style moves inspired by *Alphaville*, while giant carnivorous frogs salivated by the aqua colored kidney shaped pool. Allison barely escaped those amphibians, speeding along the coastline road into town in her Lincoln Continental convertible, the wind tousling her chlorine-tinted platinum hair.

Then Allison was in court with Cookie Flushheimer, the lawyer who handled her financial affairs. Cookie was reading a document in the front of a courtroom full of spectators: "Pursuant to the following acts on the part of protagonista Marsha Voodoo, Hostess of Mount Dümm and erstwhile Non-Dairy Kween of the people of the land of Dümmerf@kker, and antagonista Samnericka Slushpyle, Supreme Shaman-Schäme⁻ of the land of Dümmersprache, in reference to the ongoing embezzlement and misappropriation of funds by Trixie and Pissie Triglyceride, including, but not limited to, subsequent acts of philanthropic calumny by Kandie Von Krackhüren. In this regard, the opposing parties shall proceed to trial, although it remains doubtful whether, even within the bounds of the legal system of Amurycka Profunda, as it is currently defined, a rational closure of this matter will be achieved. In reference to all of the aforementioned, both parties have surrendered their weapons and have issued the following joint statement in the interest of good faith: *As the world unraveled, komodo dragons gnawed at the roots of Yggdrasil; the Blue Green Planet eventually being sucked down into the maelstrom that once was Valhaha. The Red Dwarf shall be extinguished; all remnants of that Dying Star shall be crushed inside a Singularity. "There are no Accidents in the Universe ….."*

Now Allison Eckslacks Wellness had been reincarnated as Inga-Klyngon MacFraughton, and would go on to claim first prize in the 4-H Club's Annual Søren Kierkegaard Impersonation Contest. Being that she was ill equipped to handle the pressures of success, Inga-Klyngon fell into yet another lapse of delinquency. She was mad at the world and she would make that world pay for not giving her what she thought she wanted. Inga-Klyngon tried to make the best out of a bad situation, and became renowned for tossing her hair in the manner of an insolent debu-

tante. Unfortunately, shortly after reaching this pin-
nacle of achievement, she fell into the Grim Reaper's
clutches in what was still the morning of her life. She
was accidentally decapitated by the propeller of a
helicopter on the roof of the Dubya Hotel in South
Bytch, Miasma, La Belle Floride. A recent anti-matter-
related explosion in a parallel universe had caused
the axis of the Blue Green Planet to shift ever so slightly;
just enough so that the helicopter, which was coinci-
dentally a Pornkey for the Cape Canaveral Wormhole, moved fatefully close to Inga Klyngon on her
first day of Spring Break, during the Symbionese Liber-
ation Army Karaoke Contest. Inga Klyngon's parents
donated her twenty-seven foot boa constrictor that
she had kept in an enormous Plexiglas reptile terrar-
ium enclosure, complete with special lighting in the
basement of their home, to a local sanctuary for rain-
forest creatures. The MacFraughtons, however, were
so enraged about having lost their insolent hair-toss-
ing debutante bundle of joy, that they, in an extreme
and inappropriate expression of their grief, murdered
seven employees of the South Bytch Dubya Hotel by
means of decapitation, using techniques they had

learned from watching *The Six Wives of Henry VIII* on their local public television station. At first it seemed that they would get away with their ghastly deeds, but one morning as they gazed upon the seven heads in their kitchen freezer with a serene sense of accomplishment, a SWAT team broke into their spacious and impeccable Pest Western Embalm Beach kitchen, gunning them down in the process. This sort of vigilante justice had become commonplace in Amurycka Profunda, where a combination of minarchy, Szczarya law and Evilangelism had combined to create a legal system resembling that of seventeenth century Nizhny Novgorod, Russia.

Then Allison Eckslacks Wellness was in ancient Egypt. It was 1324 B.C. and she was Two-Tank-Amen, the gay teenage Pharaoh. What a burden to have been a homosexual at that time! Fond memories included a sunny day in Memphis, sunny like most days in that city, as Two-Tank-Amen walked along a dusty main venue. Despite being an aristocrat, the peasants jeered at him: *Faggot!* Unfortunately, although he was looked upon with favor by the Hawk Headed Goddess, Two-Tank-Amen was unable to avail himself of the resources of any kind of politically correct rainbow-flag-lavender-oriented support system.

Now Allison was in the Forest of Arden, Warwickshire, England, as Rosalind from *As You Like It*, fluttering her hands and engaging in witty banter with the merry folk of the woods: *Dost thou know this place, my good fellow? This clearing with its mossy covered rocks? Why most assuredly, here is the very heart of the Kingdom of Ignorance! Where Collision + Illusion = Collusion?* All of her musings were couched in a context of delightful picnicking, charming laughter, and the magic time of late-afternoon sun filtering through the trees and down onto the brown pine needles carpeting the forest floor.

Then Allison was in a working class neighborhood in East Toronto. The sun was out on an icy winter day, and she was taking stock of her possessions in her shopping cart in the parking lot outside of Coffee Time. She was living proof that Kanadyans are not boring. She was dressed in black, dirty, ragged, spaced out, desperate. She was carrying her supply of plastic bags collected from Hasty Market and cursing at passersby at random intervals. Then Allison was in Lost Angelyst, Kali-Forn-Eye-Ay, living yet another life as a bag lady; this existence being more manageable only by virtue of the more agreeable, albeit smog-filled, climate.

Now Allison Eckslacks Wellness was in Dubai, finally a rich woman once again, relishing the good life, indulging in imported Western luxuries, five star hotels, panoramic views, the mysterious absence of a middle class, the sparkling night life of the scintillati who were oblivious to the blood on their hands. An uprising that had been brewing for months had finally come to fruition. The lower classes had had enough; they were taking back their lands. The tourists quaked with fear; the hotels had become prisons. But Alison and the rest of the jet set managed to sneak out unscathed, in just the nick of time. As she looked out from the windows of the Boeing 787 as it soared into the sky, she wondered if she would survive this trip, given that pilots with less and less experience were being paid increasingly lower wages. Below her, bombardments exploded into orange yellow desert flowers of flame. Now the plane was approaching John F. Kennedy Airport; as usual, there was the turbulence and the circling. Allison was grateful, it wouldn't be long now; but just in case, she prayed to Miyuh Hiyuh Powuh.

Then Allison Eckslacks Wellness was on Planet Vomitoria, where all the old souls wanted to be. She was in a vomitorium called Sparagmos Omophagia in Refluxia, Vomitoria's major metropolitan area. Everyone wanted to see and be seen at Sparagmos Omophagia. And everyone was relaxed, because the waters of the Chunky Peanut Butter Ocean were calm. Allison was staying near a delta that reminded her of the Nile during the time of her previous existence as Two-Tank-Amen, the gay teenage Pharaoh. Back then in ancient Egypt, shit poo mud dirt pie was considered a delicacy. She remembered how on rare rainy days, the sediment of the Nile delta was transformed into a swirl of grays, tans, browns and yellows; it metamorphosed into a chocolate vanilla marble Bedevilment's Food Blundt cake.

Allison was sitting in Café Akwarelle in Refluxia. Waiter! *Oh waiter? I'll have the sewage sludge mousse garnished with chicken claws à la Angel Heart. The waiter brought her the entrée and heaved it into her face as she had requested. Then the other patrons covered Allison like flies, and licked the sewage sludge mousse from her body, after which they slapped her until she lost consciousness. When she came to after this encounter, she felt refreshed and secure in the knowledge that all of this would soon be over and that she would soon be sent to her next incarnation. And she knew she would miss Vomitoria most of all. How I wish I could stay forever on Vomitoria, to soak in smelly steaming olive green tan mud baths! It is only then that I feel closest to Mutter Erde. Goodbye forever, Planet Vomitoria!*

Now Allison Eckslacks Wellness was back in West Whoreland, New York. Why had she been returned to this place? She had been told by her Sexually Ambiguous Life Coach, Genevieve Piss Pig, that incarnations were never repeated. Something was wrong, something was amiss. But before she could engage in any further reflection, Allison was interrupted by a shocking pain. A javelin speared her through the right eye, and then another through the left eye. And then a third and final spear caught her right in the middle of her throat. All three javelins were now embedded in the wall behind her, pinning her against that wall, the chair on which she sat balancing on its back legs precariously. There were horrible gurgling noises. Just then her husband appeared, horrified by what he was seeing. But before he could utter a word, he was decapitated by a double-edged sword. His head went bouncing out the open screen door to the porch, and then down the porch steps, where it was picked up in the jaws of the Hassenpfeffer's giant pit bull named Penny. Penny trotted off through the Hassenpfeffer's backyard with the bleeding head in her mouth, and upon seeing this, Henriette Hassenpfeffer started screaming. Meanwhile, back in the Wellness' kitchen, blood gushed out of Allison's husband's neck and his arms flailed before he collapsed on top of his dying wife.

The killer sat on the living room couch, across from the spacious and impeccable kitchen, watching the dying moments of Allison and her husband with an ecstatic, otherworldly gleam in his eyes. He resembled the sinister French albino monk from *Da Bitchy Koont*;

the only difference being that he was a Cyclops. Adrenalin surged through him as he laughed cruelly and shouted, *Blessed Be the Blayde, Chalyce, Rose and Pentackle!!!* His name was Diprivan Dulcolax (at least that was the name on his passport), and he was a fan of the Amurycka Profundan author, Bratt Beastly Alice. Diprivan began to chop up the bodies of Allison and her husband, and lay the various parts on a sheet of industrial strength plastic, where they would be drained of blood. While he was waiting to complete that procedure, he washed his hands, made some coffee, turned on the radio, and lit up a Newport. He read a lengthy article about the ongoing Middle Eastern and North African revolutions in *Newsweek* magazine. He then transferred the body parts into Glad Extra Strong 30 Gallon black trash bags and carried them down to the stand-alone freezer in the basement. He left the head of Allison in the freezer of the kitchen refrigerator, wrapped in thick translucent plastic. The presence of her head in the freezer would prove to be eventful, as the deceased couple's daughter who lived in New York City would be coming home for a visit the next day. Boy, was she ever in for a surprise!

Then Allison Eckslocks Wellness arose from an Aladdynasty lamp as a smoky frankincense Norn. She took the form of a Siberian snow leopard and walked along the roads of the Amurycka Profundan countryside in the northern part of Wyskonsyn. It was the beginning of the Dark Time in December, and as she walked, she encountered delicate glass ornaments on the path in front of her, that had been fashioned in Münszczyn, Doucheyland, in all of the traditional Christmas hues: red, green, white, silver and gold. She crushed those ornaments beneath her paws. The hide on the pads of her paw claws was tough, and therefore only minor damage was incurred by the sparkly shards of wafer-thin glass. Allison advanced along the cold moonlit blue road thinking: *So many ways to get wasted during the Dark Time! No worries, even if I land flat on my ass, there will be no judgment from my brethren in Thunder Falls, Mynnysotuh. An obscure town near the Kanadyan border, blessed with its own airport! No one will be morally conde-*

scending, and no one will try to save me if I go on a binge!

Allison proceeded to address an invisible figure in an English accent: *Yes I'll have another ladle of the finest gin punch in Christendom, Mr. Scrooge! Would it be untoward of me to refer to you as Ebenezer? In any case, I'm so glad you finally came to your senses, Mr. Scrooge, in the small window of time that remains before your death! Just try to be grateful for the abundance that you've been blessed with through all these years! Your golden idols keep you warm at night! Living on the Kamchatka Peninsula is no picnic, you know! Wyskonsyn is like La Belle Floride compared to that! Sometimes when prey is scarce, I am forced to travel to the suburbs of Vladivostok to kill humans. Yes, my hunger is sated, but then I must retreat to infamy .....*

Now Alison Eckslacks Wellness was back in human form, and back in New York City. She felt clear, serene, secure. She was walking up Chrystie Street, going from Grand towards Delancey, feeling light, hopeful, unburdened. It was one of those winter nights where the partially melted snow had refrozen due to an Arktyck Kanadyan air mass that had dropped the temperature down to 14° Fahrenheit. The snow and ice had been sculpted into amorphous shapes. Light from the streetlights reflected off this ice, and the air was still. That night Allison dreamt of a flaming Christmas tree falling off a cliff in the dark and into an abyss.

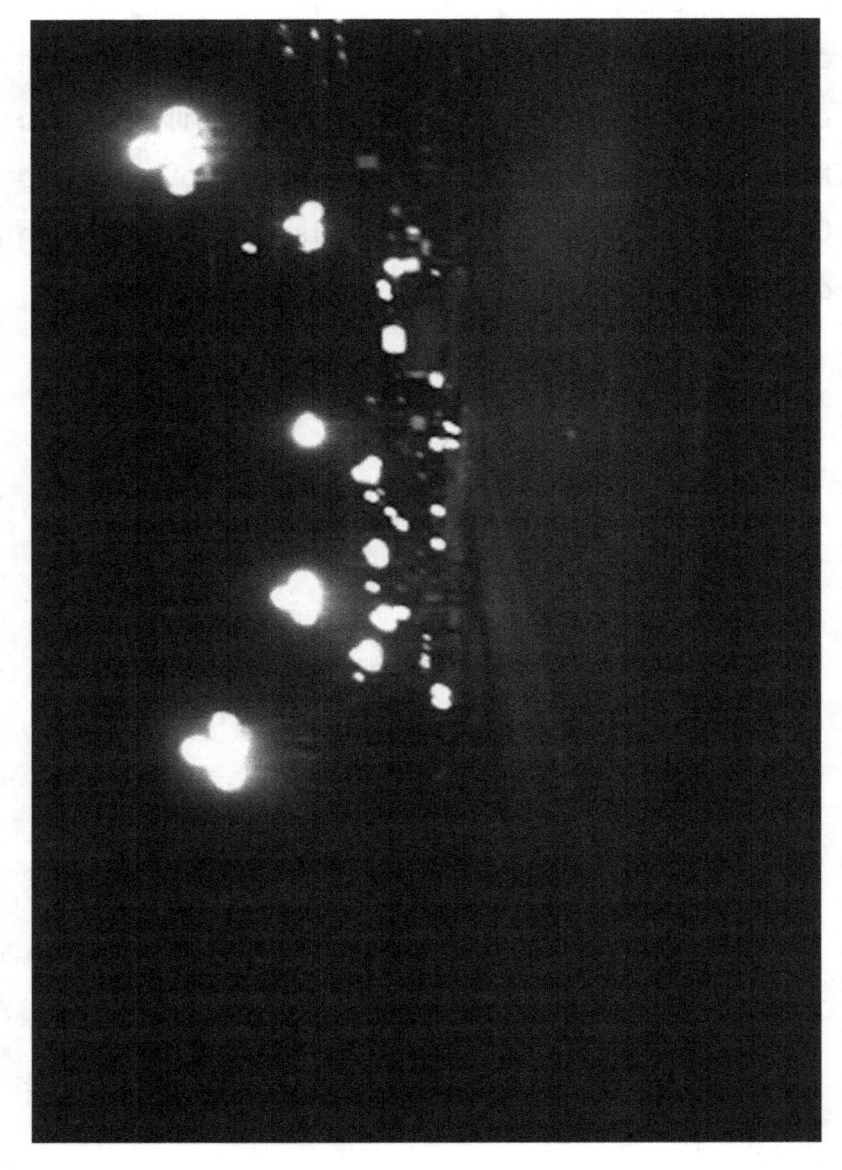

WHATEVUH HAPPENED TUH GINGER BOCEY?

How Ginger go die die?

Her fall off Griegzie Baal Tower!

Why her do that?

No one sher! Her were always a Badder, you know! Her play with fire!

Her dive off tower?

Her land flat on face. Face smash. Much blood. Then coppers draw chalk circle round body. Then coppers tape off parking lot where her land.

What were tower for?

It were from olden times when pipplez still made things with they hands!

Griegzie Baal Tower right next to old railway station bar. Me likes get wasted there!

Ginger probably met drug dealer there. Him were a Badder from Smellicottville. Then her downed much of many types of drugs with drinks. Then her climb up tower. See if her can fly! Me heard her last words was, *Dance on my grave, bitch!*

Go figure! Her were a Badder, like you says. Her took risks! Her were like La-Ura Paalm-Ur! Fyre Waalke Weethe Mee! All her life her wild! Why was things so bad for Ginger?

Her were always drunk in high school! Then her work as bartender at Wally-Whiney Hotel! Full of worse creeps than Pill Bar! Great job for her!

You make you bed you lie in it!

Not everyone make it! Some go in morning of life!

Ginger always want too much! Her always want more!

Candle go burndedie both ends! Live fast die young! No guarantee of tomorrow!

Her parents make her go burndedie? Cremate her?

Yes them make her go burndedie, then put ashes in vase, then put vase in grave!

Then us dance on grave!

That what Ginger want! That what they say, though me not hear!

Us honour her with bonfire at Aszczford Livelie Hallow Skulptur Park! First drinks at Pill Bar, then drive to Skulptur Park, then play death metal on boom box, then build bonfire, then take bath salts for be super high, then ceremonie begin!

Then us offer sky gods farts! That be Druidyck-Wyckan-Pagan!

Us burn all her shit! Us make pure with fire! Don't mean nothing now!

We pray to her gods and gods of us! We all have same gods! We pray to Lord Szczmawg, Hawk-Headed Goddess and Maya Hiyuh Powuh!

Me hope wherever Ginger is, whatever form she in, that she see us and hear us!

That what she want! She want see us and hear us! Life go on! She live on in us!

Me afraid she never knew she were loved! We will show her she were loved!

We will show her she am loved! *She will always know she be loved!*

ABOUT THE AUTHOR

Writer / performer / artist Steve Bird is the author of "Hideous Exuberance: A Satire" -- A Comic-Fantasy-Nightmare (Fiction, Vox Pop Publishing, 2009). Credits include: Readings from "Hideous Exuberance" at Notes from Underground (Von Bar), We'll Never Have Paris (107 Suffolk Street) and Barramundi; Writer / performer / producer for the one-man / variety shows Sarcastic Passion, Smirk, Ass of Satan, Superfluous Disgruntlement, Hysterical Dementia and The Socialist Variety Hour at the following venues (not respectively): New York International Fringe Festival, P. S. 122, Bowery Poets Club, Under St. Marks and Collective Unconscious (Ludlow Street). Mr. Bird is a graduate of the Gallatin School of New York University.